PAULA LENOR WEBB

Not Another Swipe

TruePair Series

Azalea City
PUBLISHING

*All things work together for the good of those who love God
and are called according to His purpose.*
Romans 8:28

Chapter 1

Barry

Barry Poet stepped off the plane into the rush of travelers at George Bush Intercontinental Airport. He noted hesitant first-time flyers and parents juggling overtired children, but continued undistracted towards baggage pick up.

He wasn't interested in the tourist shops where he saw giggly girls purchasing pink cowboy hats and matching boots. As a world traveler, the massive "Welcome to Houston" banners stretching across the terminal exit were just another sign in another place. He traveled here for a job, another mess to fix and go home.

The crowd swelled around the baggage carousel as he heard the belt rattling to life. He observed passengers jostling for position, but Barry wasn't in a rush. Instead, he scanned the terminal exit, his sniper training kicked in as his eyes caught on something unforeseen.

Barry locked in on a tall man in a black suit waiting near the exit, holding a crisp white sign: **Barry Poet**. He noticed his name in large black letters, but he hadn't rented a car and certainly not one that came with a driver.

When his black suitcase emerged from the chute, he grabbed it and approached the waiting driver. The man was likely in his fifties, his silver hair combed back with precision, and it hinted the meticulous nature within.

"Mr. Poet," the chauffeur greeted, with a slight nod. "Welcome to Houston. Your car is waiting."

Barry frowned at the unexpected attention. His years of training placed his senses on high alert. "I didn't arrange a pickup."

"No, sir," the chauffeur replied with a practiced smile. "My employer did. Mr. Eric Whiff only provides the best for his guests."

Eric Whiff. Of course. Barry ran his hand over his face in exasperation.

He exhaled slowly through his nose, a technique he learned from a holy man in India to calm his nerves. He worked with wealthy clients before; some liked to show off. He wasn't sure yet which category Whiff fell into.

"Alright," a hint of suspicion in Barry's tone. "Lead the way."

They stepped out into the brutal Houston heat, thick and heavy air, pressing down like an unwelcome hand. Barry tugged at his collar, muttering, "I'll make them all believers in the heat of hell."

The chauffeur shot a quick glance at him. "Eugene Peterson, sir?"

Barry arched a brow. A literary chauffeur. Interesting.

"Yeah," Barry shifted his grip on his bag. "I looked up Texas poets. His stuff came up."

The chauffeur chuckled as they reached the sleek black SUV idling at the curb. He opened the back door with a practiced motion and Barry slid inside.

* * *

Barry wasn't the type to fly across the country for a consultation, let alone accept ten- thousand dollars in cash, hand delivered, for an interview. He didn't chase clients; he didn't have to.

His reputation kept him booked months in advance, with high-profile figures paying top dollar for his expertise. Behind the scenes Barry maintained a specialized group that ran his operations flawlessly, keeping everyone safe. The newest member was on the following flight and used Life24/7 to track his location.

Eric Whiff went to great lengths to bring him to Houston, cutting through all the usual red tape. No haggling over rates. No tedious security screenings. Just a direct offer, the promise of discretion, and an upfront payment before he'd even agreed to the interview.

That wasn't normal.

Whiff's approach was different. The money was generous, but not flashy. The request was urgent, but not desperate. And most unusual of all, there were no strings attached.

No NDA. No contract beyond the initial deposit.

A simple text to his private client cell phone: *Come to Houston. Meet me. Decide for yourself if you want the job.*

It was enough to make Barry curious. He was between clients and was going to spend time at home in Mobile, Alabama. Maybe do a little fishing, hang out with his buddies, and talk to the cute girl at the Sandbar Sonnet. His team was also ready for a breather, but the unusual offer interested all of them.

Barry shook his head as he adjusted the cuffs of his navy blazer and ran over the specs for this possible client.

Eric Whiff.

Multi-billionaire.

Tech magnate.

Philanthropist.

Barry did his research on the flight over from his home in Mobile. Whiff wasn't just rich; he was the kind of rich that rewrote the rules. A self-made powerhouse who started with nothing and built an empire on his own terms. Business insiders hailed him as a visionary.

But for all his brilliance in business, his personal life was, to put it kindly, a mess.

Barry skimmed through the headlines in his mind.

Eric Whiff Caught Up in Another Short-Lived Romance.

Billionaire's Latest Relationship Ends in Disaster. Who's REALLY Using Who?

It didn't take a trained investigator to see the pattern. Eric Whiff had a weakness, and it wasn't money or power. He was more interested in playing the playboy with loose women and fleeting romances.

Every tabloid, gossip column, and finance blog had a theory. Some said he was naïve when it came to relationships, blind to the gold diggers and social climbers who flocked to him. Whatever the truth was, one thing was certain, Eric Whiff had no idea how to navigate his personal life with the same precision that made him a tech mogul.

And now, for some reason, he went to extraordinary lengths to hire Barry. *What did Eric Whiff need protection from?*

Barry tapped his fingers against the cool leather of the seat. Was this job about a threat? A security concern? Or was Whiff looking for someone to clean up his personal messes?

A chill ran up Barry's spine, someone was watching him. He glanced up towards the chauffeur, quiet since pulling onto the freeway, and he met Barry's eye in the rearview mirror.

"Something on your mind, sir?"

Barry studied him for a moment. The man was too polished to be only a driver. Everything about him, from his crisp posture to his measured tone, suggested he was trained for more than chauffeuring businessmen from one high-rise to another. He was a handler.

"You work for Whiff long?" Barry asked, keeping his tone casual.

"A while," the chauffeur replied smoothly.

Barry gave a half-smile. "That's not an answer."

The chauffeur's hands remained steady on the wheel. "It's the one you're getting."

Barry huffed a short breath, amused. "Alright, let's try this. What kind of man is Eric Whiff?"

A slight pause. The kind that indicated careful thought.

"The kind of man who doesn't like wasting time," the chauffeur finally replied. "Yours. Or his."

Barry arched a brow. "And yet, he paid me ten grand just to show up."

The chauffeur smiled faintly. "Consider it an investment. Mr. Whiff values expertise. He also values efficiency. If you weren't worth his time, you wouldn't be in this car."

Barry absorbed the information. The answer was crafted, measured, revealing enough to intrigue, but not enough to expose.

"You're good at this," Barry said.

"At what, sir?"

"Dodging questions."

The chauffeur met his gaze briefly in the mirror. "It's not dodging, Mr. Poet. It's discretion."

Barry raised the corner of his mouth as he suppressed a laugh.

"Alright, one more," Barry said. "What does Whiff need from me?"

The chauffeur made a slow turn, guiding the SUV off the freeway and onto the city streets. "That," he said smoothly, "is something only Mr. Whiff can tell you."

Barry sat back, exhaling through his nose. Clever. The man answered without answering.

Barry adjusted his cuff again. The city skyline loomed ahead, golden in the afternoon sun. His gut told him this wasn't just another job.

And for a man like him, that was either a good thing, or not.

* * *

Barry didn't like the idea of playing babysitter to a billionaire with poor judgment. But as he sat in the reception room, sipping expensive tea and waiting for Whiff, he knew the timing was too perfect to ignore. Ten thousand dollars cash went a long way toward helping his old friend, Caleb Tolmin, get back on his feet. This wasn't another job, it was an opportunity he could not pass up.

Caleb, one of the best lawyers in Mobile, struggled for months, living alone in a rundown beach house along Mobile Bay that belonged to his family before the Civil War. The salt air had eaten through the wooden siding, the porch sagged like an old man's back, and the roof barely kept the rain out. He and his wife were going to renovate the place and return it to its former splendor – but that didn't happen.

Worse than the house, though, was the way Caleb was unraveling. Ever since losing his wife to a "car accident," he was a ghost of himself, drinking too much, talking too little, and teetering on the edge of losing everything, including his law practice and mind. Barry tried to help before, but pride was a stubborn thing, and Caleb never took handouts. The team agreed to use the money to help Caleb.

A voice, smooth as silk and laced with professionalism, interrupted his thoughts.

"Mr. Poet, Mr. Whiff is ready for you now."

Barry glanced up, meeting the assistant's gaze. She was stunning, sleek dark hair pulled into a sophisticated twist, high cheekbones accentuated by subtle makeup, and a crisp white blouse tucked into a fitted pencil skirt. Her eyes, an unreadable shade of hazel, studied him with polite detachment, as if she saw men like him before and wasn't impressed.

As they reached the end of the corridor, the assistant paused, then pushed open a pair of frosted glass doors with effortless grace. The office beyond was a display of quiet luxury with its floor-to-ceiling windows revealed a breathtaking view of the city, the skyline stretching endlessly.

A long, modern desk of sleek white marble sat in the center of the room. As Barry walked into the office, he caught a subtle hint of leather and citrus, the unmistakable sign of an environment meticulously maintained. It was a place where every detail mattered.

Eric Whiff stood near the window, one hand tucked casually in his pocket, the other spinning a pen between his fingers. He turned as they entered, a slow, easy grin spreading across his face. He was younger than Barry had expected, late thirties at most, with sharp, aristocratic features that hinted at new money.

Despite the carefully curated image of laid-back confidence, Barry spent enough time around powerful men to recognize when one carried unseen weight. There was something in Eric's eyes, not quite exhaustion, not quite distrust, but something that spoke of a man who had everything yet incomplete. It didn't match the reputation Barry read about, the so-called billionaire bachelor rogue with an instinct for making money, a revolving door of arm candy, and an ability to turn bad deals into gold.

The assistant stepped aside, her job done, and Barry took a few steps forward, this meeting more interesting than anticipated.

Barry watched Eric Whiff study him, his expression unreadable before a curve crossed his lips. "Barry Poet. The man, the myth, the guy who supposedly doesn't take meetings like this."

Barry folded his arms, deadpan. "And yet, here I am. Either I have terrible judgment, or you made me an offer I couldn't refuse."

Eric's grin widened. "Let's hope it's the latter."

Barry extended his hand, and Eric shook it. As they released, his sharp eyes scanned the room like muscle memory, taking stock of everything including the single security camera in the corner, the lack of personal photographs, the curated, high-end furniture. Everything about the office screamed precision and control.

The camera is too obvious, there must be so much tech in this place, he didn't need a physical bodyguard till now. What has changed?

Then he glanced at Eric again, the billionaire in a t-shirt, jeans, and sneakers.

"…Though, judging by your outfit, I might need to reconsider."

Eric snorted. "What? You were expecting a tuxedo?"

"Let's just say I wasn't expecting someone who just came from a gaming convention, Mr. Sandler."

Eric clutched his chest in mock offense. "I'll have you know, this is a limited-edition shirt that costs more than your suit."

Barry smirked. "And yet, I still look like the professional in the room."

* * *

"Please, sit," Eric gestured toward a low leather chair.

Barry hesitated for half a second then lowered himself, letting it absorb his weight. Eric, on the other hand, sprawled into his seat like a man exhausted by his own existence.

"I won't waste your time," Eric's fingers drumming against the armrest. "I need someone who can protect me, not just from threats to my safety, but…" He exhaled sharply, dragging a hand through his already-mussed hair. "…from myself."

Barry gave him a flat look. "You want me to guard you from *you*? That's a new one."

Eric let out a dry laugh, shaking his head. "Yeah. Crazy, right? But you know who I am. Hell, *everyone* knows who I am. My love life is a damn disaster, and it's playing out on a national stage. I can build a multi-billion-dollar empire from nothing, negotiate circles around CEOs who've been in the game for decades, but put me in a room with a beautiful woman, and suddenly I have the decision-making skills of a hormonal teenager."

Barry raised an eyebrow. "You said it, not me."

Eric sighed, rubbing a hand over his jaw. "I keep chasing unsuitable women. Over and over. I know it. My board knows it. The entire *world* knows it. I see the headlines. *'Eric Whiff's Latest Flame, Love or Gold Digging?' 'Tech Titan's Love Life: A Masterclass in Bad Decisions.'* Even my own advisors treat me like a headstrong kid who can't be trusted with his personal life."

He let out a frustrated huff, leaning back. "I need someone who will call me out before I make another mistake. Someone who'll tell me, *hey, idiot, she's only laughing at your jokes because you're a rich guy.* I have this new girl I am seeing, Crystal Shanda Lier, everyone is saying she is like the others, but I can't tell."

Barry leaned back in his chair arms crossed. "So, what you're saying is you don't need protection. You need parenting."

Eric groaned. "Please, don't say that. It makes it sound worse, but really, I need both. We are about to premiere a new train and rail system, and we are already getting threats. My current bodyguard is on another assignment."

Barry met his gaze steadily. "You want me to keep you out of trouble? I need to call it what it is."

Eric pointed at him. "See, that? That's what I need. Someone who's not afraid to tell me when I'm about to walk into a disaster."

Barry exhaled through his nose. He'd dealt with high-profile clients before, but this? This was going to be something else entirely.

"Alright," Barry said finally. "Let's talk terms."

Eric sat forward, resting his elbows on his knees. "Before we get into specifics, I need to know, are you interested? Because if this sounds like a job beneath you, I'd rather find out now."

Barry exhaled slowly, eyes sweeping the office again observing no personal touches, just clean lines, expensive furniture, and a view that screamed power. Yet, the man in front of him was a mess, even if he hid it well.

"I'll admit," Barry said as he adjusted his watch, "this isn't my usual kind of job. But I know one thing, you're willing to throw a hell of a lot of money at a problem most people could solve with common sense."

Eric scoffed. "Oh, *please.* If it were that simple, I wouldn't have half the media waiting to pounce on my next disaster. You think I *enjoy* being the punchline to every billionaire playboy joke? I need someone with instincts. Someone who can see the mess coming before I step in it."

Barry studied him. Eric wasn't throwing money at a vanity project and he knew he had a problem. That put him one step ahead of most of the rich idiots Barry dealt with.

"Alright," Barry nodded. "You need someone to help you navigate your personal life before it turns into another front-page spectacle. I can do that. But I don't do micromanaging. If you want me to do my job, you listen when I tell you to walk away from a bad situation. You might say yes now but what about when I tell you no?"

Eric chuckled. "Fair enough." He leaned back, rubbing his hands together. "So, let's talk numbers."

Barry knew the pay would be obscene and had visions of improving the technology his team used for surveillance. That wasn't the issue. The real question was how much of his sanity this job was going to cost him. What Eric didn't know and what Barry wasn't about to volunteer was that he never worked alone. His team was small, quiet, smart and if this job went sideways, he would need all of them.

"I need full autonomy," Barry said. "If I say someone's a problem, you don't argue. And I want final say on security, if I need more people, you pay."

Eric nodded. "Fine. Anything else?"

Barry hesitated, then added, "This is short-term. A few months, tops. I'm not making Houston my permanent home."

Eric raised an eyebrow. "Not a fan of the city?"

"It's fine," Barry said with a shrug. "But I have a life back in Alabama, and I don't plan on giving it up to manage yours long-term."

Eric smirked. "Fair enough."

Barry just shook his head. "Nothing without my approval. Not even yacht parties."

Eric groaned. "You sound like my accountant."

"I'll take that as a compliment." Barry leaned forward, extending his hand again. "You've got yourself a deal."

Eric grasped it, shaking firmly. "Welcome to the circus."

Barry had no doubt this was going to be one hell of a ride.

* * *

Barry was in Houston for less than twenty-four hours, and he questioned his life choices.

Coffee. Must have coffee.

The city was fine, good food, decent weather, too many tech bros everywhere he looked but Barry didn't plan to stay long.

He needed Eric Whiff to get his personal life under control, keep him out of the headlines, and then he was out. He checked Live 24/7 to see that Aidan Brooks, the latest member of his team, had arrived safely and was at a low-key Airbnb a few blocks away from both Eric's office and penthouse.

But first, he needed coffee. Good coffee.

He found a spot near the University of Houston campus called Moody Grounds, one of those indie cafés with mismatched furniture, exposed brick walls, and baristas who looked like they spent their free time writing existential poetry. The waiting line was long, but caffeine was non-negotiable.

Perfect.

A voice from the front of the line cut through the low murmur of the shop. "This is not what I ordered."

Barry stepped to the side to get a better view. The woman at the counter stood with her arms crossed, lips pressed tight. She wasn't loud, but there was an edge to her voice, sharp, precise, like someone used to being right and absolutely unwilling to let this slide.

"I asked for an *iced brown sugar oat milk shaken espresso with salted caramel cold foam*. This is…" She tilted the cup, unimpressed. "…whatever this is."

The barista, a college kid who looked like he'd rather be anywhere else, blinked at the cup in his hand. "Uh, that's an iced latte."

She exhaled through her nose. "Right. And that's *not* what I ordered."

The kid shrugged. "I mean… it's kinda the same thing."

Barry let out a quiet snort. *The wrong answer, kid.*

The woman's eyes narrowed like a predator locking onto its prey. "Oh, is it? Would you like to pay six dollars for a drink you didn't want?"

The barista glanced around, seeking an escape route.

Before things could escalate, Barry stepped forward. "Hey, if she doesn't want the drink, I'll take it."

She turned to him, blinking in surprise. "You drink… that?"

Barry eyed the cup. He had no idea what was in it, but it looked more milk than coffee. Not his usual black.

"Sure," he said with a shrug. "Why not? I have had worse."

The barista, clearly relieved, shoved the drink toward Barry. "Alright, man. It's yours."

Barry took a slow sip. Sweet. Way too sweet. He grimaced slightly but powered through.

The woman raised an eyebrow. "You hate it."

Barry smirked. "No, I *strongly dislike* it. But I got to cut the line, I have coffee, so I call that a win."

To his surprise, a small smile tugged at her lips. "Well, enjoy your completely incorrect version of an *iced brown sugar oat milk shaken espresso with salted caramel cold foam*."

"I'll do my best," he said, then nodded toward the barista. "Now let's see if this kid can actually get yours right."

She sighed but turned back to the counter, clearly still annoyed but less so.

Barry took another sip of his overly sweet drink and watched her out of the corner of his eye. There was something about her, sharp, but not unkind.

As he left the coffee shop to return to the world of Whiff, he pulled out the small notebook tucked inside his jacket and made a note: *Moody Grounds. Coffee. Brown curls. Precise tone. No nonsense.* She was one of those random people that stuck in one's memory.

Chapter 2

Claire

Claire Eidean pushed open the coffee shop door and stepped out into the warm Texas air. She sipped her favorite, iced brown sugar oat milk shaken espresso with salted caramel foam, as her mind drifted back to the man who hijacked her ruined drink. There was something about him, nice smile, sharp wit, the way he carried himself, that lingered.

She walked through the grand front doors of the historic Perry Library on the university campus, nodding to Zak behind the circulation desk. The bell tower chimed overhead as she took the stairs to her second-floor office, her coffee in hand and thoughts still half caught on that stranger.

Claire flicked on the office light and immediately spotted the framed photo of her with Sam.

Ugg. I should put it away, but I'm not ready for people to ask questions. Too humiliating. She lightly touched the frame, as if Sam might magically reappear in her life.

For five years, she'd found an anchor in Sam Ellis, a fellow academic in the university's history department. They'd shared everything, books, quiet nights over coffee, and traveled together when their schedules aligned. She'd thought they were building something lasting, a future rooted in learning and life in Houston.

Yet, despite her efforts to merge their lives by sharing an apartment or house, he found a reason not to take the final step. One time she stayed over and slipped her toothbrush into the holder in the bathroom as a quiet hint, but nothing changed. She ignored the signs, she should have known better, and now he was a memory.

Everything shifted when Sam got the offer. A tenure-track position at Stanford, one of the most prestigious universities in the country. She remembered the way he'd hesitated before telling her, as if he was bracing for impact, trying to soften the blow.

"It's a once-in-a-lifetime opportunity," he said not able to meet her gaze as he sat across from her at Moody Grounds. His fingers had nervously toyed with the edge of his mug. "I can't pass it up, Claire. You understand, right?"

Internally, she felt something crumble when she heard those words a quiet collapse, like a bridge giving way under too much weight.

At the time, she'd told him she understood, said it to make things easier. They could make it work. She flew out to California a handful of times, trying to convince herself. But as the months passed, the phone calls grew shorter, the texts less frequent. The connection they'd once shared unraveled, thread by thread, until there was nothing left but polite goodbyes and a handful of unanswered emails.

She left her office and stepped into the main part of the library, letting the cool, familiar air wrap around her. The quiet, the students and the orderly rows of books were comforting, a rhythm she relied on.

Claire loved her work, helping students find the right resources, organizing the collection, and ensuring the library remained a place of discovery. But today, her mind kept drifting back to that brief conversation with the stranger, the exchange that had felt both frustrating and oddly intriguing.

Claire pushed the cart down the library's main aisle, her heels clicking softly against the polished floor. She paused to straighten a display of new arrivals, smoothing her hands over the spines of freshly bound books. After things with Sam ended, she'd thrown herself into her work. It was easier to organize information than emotions, easier to catalog a collection than to sort through her own regrets.

Her thoughts were interrupted by the soft chime of the library's front doors. Claire glanced up automatically, her practiced smile already in place.

A young couple walked in; their fingers entwined as they juggled a small pile of textbooks. They were laughing softly, the sound carrying through the stillness. As they passed, the girl leaned toward the boy, her expression tender, and the boy answered with a look that could only be described as adoration.

Claire watched them, her smile faltering. A lump rose in her throat, heavy and suffocating. She looked away quickly, her chest tightening with an ache she hadn't let herself feel in a long time.

She told herself she didn't need that, not the handholding, the soft glances, the shared secrets. She convinced herself that love was a luxury she could live without, that independence was enough. She spent years being the strong one in her family, the dependable daughter, the quiet fixer. The truth gnawed at her; a hollow ache buried beneath years of pretending she was fine.

Didn't she want someone to look at her that way? Didn't she deserve it, too?

When she turned back to her cart, something inside her whispered otherwise. It wasn't just about missing companionship, it was about wanting to be seen, to be cherished, to have someone reach for her hand in the way that boy reached for the girl's. She wasn't ready to give up on love, not yet. A piece of her was full of hope, longing for something more.

Claire sighed, her gaze lingering on the cart of books in front of her. She hadn't thought about relationships since it ended with Sam. It was easier to bury herself at work, to pretend she was better off alone. But maybe… maybe she wasn't as fine as she told herself.

As she returned to her cart she saw a new release of poems by Christina Rossetti, one of her favorite poets, and one of them drifted into her mind, unbidden.

Sometimes I said, "This thing shall be no more;
My expectation wearies and shall cease;
I will resign it now and be at peace:"

She wasn't ready to become the single, crazy cat librarian lady yet. But maybe, just maybe, she was willing to try one more time.

* * *

The sound of children shouting echoed down the hallway as Claire pushed open the front door of her childhood home. The familiar creak of the hinges brought a bittersweet pang to her chest. It was a sharp ache of nostalgia and regret. Once, this house was a sanctuary of warmth and quiet routines. Now, with its scuffed floors and faded wallpaper, it resembled a storm barely contained by its walls.

"Claire! You're here!" Camila's voice rang out.

Claire dropped her bag by the door and stepped into the kitchen. Camila was furiously wiping down the counter while her three kids argued over a tablet at the island, their voices rising like a chaotic choir.

And then there was Charles Crudd, Camilia's husband.

Fully outfitted in a vintage Star Trek science officer uniform, complete with boots, communicator badge, and a too-serious expression, he sat at the kitchen table full of stuff from their latest grocery haul, unbothered by the domestic hurricane swirling around him.

Claire stopped in her tracks. "Please tell me that's not your idea of lounge wear."

Charles looked up and grinned. "Just got back from CosmicFest. The panel on transporter ethics ran late, but it was worth it."

Claire raised an eyebrow. "So, Starfleet is here to negotiate snacks?"

Camila waved a hand. "You know he runs vendor booths for those things. They don't need him right now, so he's home 'helping.'"

Claire gave her sister a long look. "Define helping."

Charles stood and adjusted his insignia. "I've already reorganized the pantry by galaxy. Earth snacks top shelf. Klingon treats… TBD."

Before Claire could respond, Camila glanced up and gave her a quick hug, her tone brisk. "Good timing. Mom is in her room. I got her settled after her physical therapy this afternoon."

"Thanks for handling things," Claire said.

Camila snorted. "Who else is going to do it? You're too busy with your librarian life, and Chloe's who-knows-where. Have you heard from her? She skipped out on us. I knew that guy was trouble. She left us, Claire, you know that, right? She didn't even say goodbye. We are supposed to pretend this is normal?"

Claire ignored the jab towards their absent sister and made her way down the hall to her mother's room. The air grew quieter as she approached, muffled by the hum of the portable air purifier Charles had set up last year.

Beatrice Eidean lay propped up in bed, her thin frame nestled by the pile of pillows. Her once-vibrant blue eyes lit up at the sight of Claire.

"Hello, my love," she whispered.

"Hey, Mom," Claire said softly, easing in the chair beside the bed. She reached for her mother's hand, which trembled but warmed as Claire held it. "You look good today. Did the therapy go okay?"

Beatrice nodded her head.

Claire fought back the sting of tears as her mother strained with the simplest of movements. It wasn't fair. The woman who once was a force of nature, who held their family together, was now a fragile shell. And Claire, despite all her efforts, could do nothing but witness as time stole her away.

Later that evening, as she sat in her quiet apartment, Claire's phone buzzed. She glanced at the screen to see Chloe's name light up.

Hey, sis. Just checking in. How's Mom?

Claire hesitated before typing back.

She's hanging in there. Same as always. How are you?

Good. Traveling a bit. I'll call soon. Love you.

Love you too, Claire replied, staring at the screen long after the message disappeared. Any questions were pointless, because Chloe never gave straight answers, always one foot out the door.

She didn't tell Camila. It wasn't worth the drama. Chloe did what Claire secretly wished to do and leave the chaos behind. Claire wasn't sure she'd ever have the courage to do the same.

* * *

Claire tapped the call button and held her phone to her ear, pacing her small apartment as it rang. Oliver, her butterball of a cat, watched her intently as she paced. It wasn't time for his supper yet, but he looked for every opportunity.

She hated calling Camila, it always ended in guilt or sarcasm, but she needed to be certain the money she'd sent went to the right place. If it hadn't, she wouldn't be surprised. It was exhausting. While her sister was good with her mother's accounts, she tended to view Claire's financial contributions as chump change.

"Hello?" Camila answered.

"It's me," Claire said. "Just wanted to check that you got the transfer. And Mom has her meds."

Camila sighed dramatically. "Yes, Claire, we got it. Charles is picking up the meds tomorrow."

"Good," Claire said, relieved. "I just wanted to be sure."

"Wait," Camila interrupted, her voice sharpening with interest. "What's going on with you and that professor? When are you finally going to tie the knot? He must be making bank at Samford."

Claire winced. She dreaded this question. She tightened her grip on the phone, looked at Oliver as if he might give her an excuse to go, but then took a steady breath, and decided to rip off the Band-Aid.

"We broke up," Claire said.

The silence on the other end of the line was deafening. Then, predictably, Camila erupted.

"What?" she screeched. "Oh, Claire! Seriously? What is wrong with you? You dated that man for five years! FIVE YEARS! And now you're casually telling me it's over? Why didn't you tell me sooner?"

"It's been over for a while," Claire said quietly.

"Well, that's just great," Camila snapped, her voice dripping with sarcasm. "You're going to end up a spinster. Charles! Did you hear this? Claire broke up with that professor!"

Claire cringed as she heard Charles's muffled response in the background, something like, "Beam me up, Scotty."

"Camila, I don't need the commentary," Claire said, trying to keep her voice even.

"Oh, don't worry, Charles knows a guy," Camila said, breezing right past her. "He works with him at Comic-vendors. He's nice! Single. Hardworking. You should meet him. Though he does have an affinity for Star Wars. Think you can dress up as Princess Leia?"

"Absolutely not," Claire said, shaking her head even though Camila couldn't see her.

Camila clicked her tongue. "See, that's your problem, Claire. You're too uppity. Always have been. You think you're better than the rest of us, with your books and your degrees. You need to stop being so picky. You're not getting any younger, you know."

"Camila, I, "

"And you're not exactly Miss America," Camila continued mercilessly. "If you want kids, you don't have time to be picky."

Claire pressed a hand to her forehead, her face burning with embarrassment.

Then Camila's voice dropped to a conspiratorial whisper. "Or… maybe you like girls? It's okay if you do, you know. You can tell me."

Claire's cheeks burned hotter. "I'm not attracted to women, Camila. There's nothing wrong with it, but that's not me. I just haven't found the right man yet."

Camila burst into laughter. "Oh, Claire. You're so naive. There's no such thing as the 'right man.' You pick one, and you deal with his nonsense."

In the background, the sound of multiple taser blasts echoed through the phone.

"See what I mean?" Camila said, laughing harder.

Claire closed her eyes and pinched the bridge of her nose. "Thanks for the advice, Camila. I've got to go now."

"Suit yourself," Camila said breezily. "But don't say I didn't warn you when you're old and alone with your books and cat."

Claire tossed her phone onto the couch with a frustrated sigh. She loved her sister, but sometimes talking to Camila was like walking into a verbal buzzsaw.

She sank into the cushions, staring at the ceiling. She knew Camila wasn't completely wrong. But that didn't mean Claire was ready to settle for someone who didn't make her heart sing, no matter how unlikely Camila thought that was.

A knock came at her front door and Oliver ran to her bedroom, hiding in the closet.

Strange, I wasn't expecting anyone.

She got up from the couch and looked out the peephole.

No one was there.

* * *

Claire adjusted the stack of books in her arms as she moved down the main corridor of Perry Library. The late afternoon light streamed through the tall windows, casting golden patterns across the polished floor. She truly loved this place.

The library settled into its usual rhythm, pages turning, muffled steps, the quiet hum of intellectual pursuit.

Then she saw them again, the young couple. She noticed them before, always wrapped in their own world, reality blurred at the edges. They arrived hand in hand, their laughter soft and unguarded, the kind that hinted at inside jokes and whispered confessions.

And sex, she thought, *Lots of good young sex.*

Without breaking stride, they disappeared into the waiting elevator, the doors sliding shut with a gentle chime.

Claire stood still for a moment, watching the empty space where they were. There was something magnetic about the ease between them, an effortless intimacy she wasn't sure she had ever experienced. A dull ache settled in her heart, but she dismissed it before it could take root.

As she turned towards the front desk, a small, white rectangle caught her eye. It lay near the entrance, half-hidden against the tile floor. She bent down, balancing her books with one arm, and picked it up.

The card was simple but elegant, its soft blue lettering crisp against the matte surface:

Find the one who truly gets you.

TruePair: Real matches for real people.

Below the tagline, a bold line stood out:

One-week free access. Use code TRUELOVE at sign-up. No credit card is required.

Claire ran her thumb over the edge of the card, hesitating. Then, without overthinking it, she slipped it into her pocket. Maybe it was curiosity. Maybe it was the universe's odd sense of timing. Or maybe she was tired of telling herself she didn't care. Her heart skipped.

Later that evening, Claire sat cross-legged on her couch, a cooling mug of her coffee resting on the coffee table. The library long since closed, and the quiet of her apartment wrapped around her like a well-worn sweater.

She reached into her pocket and pulled out the card, turning it over between her fingers.

One week free. No strings attached.

It wasn't as if she hadn't considered online dating. Camila scoffed at her situation earlier that week, dismissing her as an old-fashioned romantic stuck in the past. *"If you're waiting for some grand, meet-cute moment, Claire, you'll be waiting forever."*

Camila was wrong. She wasn't waiting. She stopped believing it was worth the effort.

But this? Perhaps a trial run, a way to peek through the window without stepping inside.

Before she could talk herself out of it, Claire opened her laptop and typed the website into her browser. The homepage was sleek and inviting, the same tagline from the card displayed in soft, modern typography:

Find the one who truly gets you.

Her cursor hovered over the sign-up button. Was she really doing this? *It's just one week. What's the harm?*

She entered the promo code and was immediately pulled into a series of questions that went deeper than she expected.

What makes you happiest?

How do you handle conflict?

What are you looking for in a partner?

They weren't shallow prompts begging a list of hobbies and favorite movies. They forced her to pause; to consider the things she hadn't put into words in years.

By the time she reached the profile photo section, Claire's fingers hovered over her camera roll. She scrolled past snapshots from her sister's last chaotic family gathering, a few scattered shots of old library events, and then, one caught her eye.

A self-portrait taken during a rainy afternoon. One of her student assistants needed a portrait for an art project and Claire agreed to help. Her face was partially obscured by the tilt of an umbrella, her profile barely visible against the blur of falling raindrops. Thoughtful. Neutral. Just enough to be her, without truly revealing herself.

This will do.

She uploaded the photo.

Then came the final step.

Name:

She hesitated, her fingers flexing over the keyboard before typing:

Emma Green.

Emma, for her favorite literary heroine. Green, because it was her lawyer's last name and he was one of the best people she knew, familiar, but not hers.

She scanned everything one last time. No real identifiers. No ties to Claire Eidean, an academic librarian.

With a deep breath, she clicked **Submit**.

The screen refreshed:

Welcome to TruePair! Your profile is live. Matches will appear soon.

Claire exhaled, leaning back against the couch, her pulse oddly unsteady.

She wasn't Claire Eidean, overworked librarian with a complicated family and no patience for modern romance.

She was Emma Green.

For one week, at least.

Now, all she could do was wait.

Chapter 3

Barry

Barry recalled Eric's concerns about Crystal as he watched the woman sashay through the penthouse door, her red-bottomed platform heels clicking sharply against the marble floor like a metronome.

She was striking, easily over six feet in those towering heels, with long, perfectly styled platinum-blonde hair cascading down her back like a waterfall of light. Her outfit was impossible to miss head-to-toe hot pink, from her cropped designer jacket to the skintight, ruched mini dress that clung to every curve like a second skin. Even her oversized sunglasses, which she didn't bother removing indoors, had a rose-tinted hue that mirrored the gleaming clutch tucked under her arm.

Barry saw characters moving in and out of the suite in Eric's penthouse, but Crystal? She was in a category all her own. Like a walking magazine spread, part fashion model, part fire hazard. And judging by the way she paused in the foyer, slowly panning the room as if measuring it for renovations, she knew it.

And yet, beneath all that glamour, Barry noticed something else. Her eyes—what little he could see of them behind the pink gradient lenses—were scanning, calculating. Not just posing. Observing. Maybe Eric had a reason to worry.

Humm...she certainly wants to be noticed. Barry observed as he sent a text to Aidan to begin a background check on her.

It wasn't Crystal's attitude that was out of place. What startled him was the way Eric bounded behind her as an overexcited puppy. "Barry, meet Crystal Shanda Lier. Crystal, this is Barry Poet, my new bodyguard."

Crystal gave Barry a once-over, her glossy lips curling into a sneer. "A bodyguard, huh? Looks more like a bouncer."

Barry kept his expression neutral, but his instincts were on high alert. There was something off about her, and was a little too dismissive.

She strutted further into the penthouse, tossing her designer handbag, also pink, onto the marble counter as if she owned the place. Barry noted the way she surveyed her surroundings, calculating, appraising. She was comfortable here, too cozy as if she claimed her stake.

"Eric, babe," Crystal cooed, turning her attention back to her boyfriend. "I was thinking, since you're such a sweetie, you could send me and the girls to Cabo for the weekend. We could totally use the jet. Don't you think?"

Barry didn't flinch, but he clocked the way she fluttered her lashes and leaned in close, her voice dripped with fake sweetness as she gave Eric a peek down her top. His face reddened as he nodded.

"Yeah, of course. Whatever you want," Eric grinned.

Crystal grabbed Eric by the collar, fell into his lap, and pulled him into a deep, possessive kiss, her lips claiming his in front of Barry with an unmistakable message.

Barry kept his face blank. *Goodness, she looks like an octopus going in for the kill.*

The display was bold, intentional, and dripping with ownership. "You're the best, babe." Then, ignoring Barry, she breezed out the door calling over her shoulder, "Text me the details, okay? I will see you tonight."

Barry exhaled slowly, shaking his head. "Love looks not with the eyes, but with the mind, and therefore is winged Cupid painted blind." He muttered, quoting Shakespeare. He waited until the door shut before speaking. "So... that's Crystal?"

Eric ran a hand through his hair, a sheepish grin on his face. "She's great, right? Beautiful, smart, fun…"

Barry raised an eyebrow. "And expensive."

Eric chuckled. "She's worth it. Tonight is going to be amazing."

Barry folded his arms, leaning against the wall. "Is she? Or is she just the latest in a long line of women bleeding you dry? If you are that desperate, there are other ways to blow your money with no commitment."

Eric flinched at the bluntness but didn't argue.

"Look," Barry continued, his tone softer but firm. "I'm not here to judge your life, but I've been doing this job long enough to spot a grifter when I see one. That girl? She's not here for you. She's here for what you can give her. Has she asked you anything about your rail project? Be careful with that one."

Eric sighed, sinking onto the couch. "You don't understand, Barry. I'm not good at… this. At relationships. My dad wasn't either. He raised me alone after my mom died. She was amazing, at least from what I remember. But after she was gone, it was us. He taught me how to work hard, how to make money. Not how to deal with women."

Barry stayed quiet, letting Eric get it out.

"I've always thought if I just give them everything they want, they have a good time and I'll have a good time," Eric admitted, his voice low. "But it never works, does it?"

"No," Barry said evenly. "It doesn't. The right person doesn't care about your money, Eric. They care about you. You're a good guy, but you're using people, and they are using you right back."

Eric looked up at Barry, his expression torn between frustration and gratitude. "You are telling me the truth? You think I am a good person? Wow. So, what do I do?"

Barry shrugged. "Start by saying no. To her, to anyone who doesn't appreciate you for who you are. You don't need a bodyguard for your wallet. You need one for your heart."

Eric laughed, "That's a bit poetic, don't you think?"

Barry shrugged. "It's in the name."

He pushed off the wall and made his way to his assigned suite, tucked in the guest wing of Eric's sprawling Houston penthouse. It was spacious, outfitted with sleek furniture and neutral tones that felt more curated than lived in. The bed was large and plush, but Barry did not sleep much; always half-alert, attuned to his job.

The bathroom was pristine, outfitted with high-end toiletries he never used. He could disassemble and reassemble his pistol in five minutes, but the remote to the toilet was beyond his expertise. He sheepishly asked one of the maids to show him how to flush.

There was a walk-in closet bigger than the apartments he'd lived in, mostly empty except for his neatly arranged suits and a duffel bag perpetually packed, ready to go at a moment's notice. The space was nice, more than nice, but it wasn't his.

He lived in worse places, sure, but something about living under Eric's roof left him restless. It wasn't only the space, it was the sense of detachment and no matter how long he stayed, he didn't belong here. It was too polished, too impersonal, like a luxury showroom instead of a home.

He wasn't here for pampering.

Barry was here to do a job. And that meant keeping an eye on people like Crystal, who marked her territory with a well-manicured hand.

Feeling the need for distraction, Barry wandered into Eric's personal library, a large, lavish room lined with bookshelves filled with a wide variety of 18th and 19th-century antiques and pristine, untouched volumes of books. He noted the beautiful designs on the spines as his fingers traced the images until he pulled out a dusty copy of *Bartlett's Book of Quotations*. He smirked at the irony, flipping through the pages until he found a passage that fit the situation perfectly.

'The world is full of fools and faint hearts;
and yet everyone has courage enough to bear the misfortunes,
and wisdom enough to manage the affairs, of his neighbor.'
Barry muttered under his breath, closing the book with a quiet snap.

* * *

Barry lingered in a chair off to the side as Eric sat at the head of the sleek, black-glass conference table. The skyline of Houston glimmered behind him through his main office's floor-to-ceiling windows, but no one in the room was paying attention to the view.

A faint air of impatience radiated from both men. Eric with his signature stillness that suggested barely concealed calculation, and Barry, whose arms were crossed, chair tilted back against the wall, legs casually extended but eyes constantly moving. He wasn't just a bystander. He was scanning for tells, for shifts in tone, for anything that didn't add up.

Across the table, two presenters sat side by side. The man, mid-thirties, nervous energy bundled into a too-tight gray suit, cleared his throat and leaned slightly forward. He adjusted his glasses with a jittery flick of his fingers, trying to mask the tremor in his voice.

"Mr. Whiff," he began, forcing a smile, "TruePair isn't your standard dating app. It's built on cutting-edge psychological algorithms and the latest AI research in personality compatibility. We're talking about perfect matches, guaranteed."

Eric's fingers tapped once against the armrest of his chair. He arched an eyebrow, just slightly. "Perfect matches? That's a bold claim."

Before the man could respond, the woman beside him, Sasha Langford, interjected smoothly. She radiated calm, her poise in stark contrast to her colleague's anxious energy. With sharp cheekbones, a high ponytail, and a tailored navy blazer over a silk blouse, she looked every inch the woman who didn't waste words or time.

"Our proprietary system has a success rate of ninety-four percent in early trials," she said, folding her hands atop the portfolio in front of her. "It doesn't just pair users based on shared interests or hobbies. It analyzes communication styles, conflict responses, even attachment theory patterns. We're not offering casual swipes. We're creating the foundation for deep, lasting connection."

Barry's brows lifted ever so slightly. That last line rang familiar. Too familiar. He cut his eyes toward Eric, who was nodding thoughtfully but wore the expression Barry recognized as: I'm listening, but you haven't impressed me yet.

"Let's say I invest," Eric said, his voice low, calculated. "What's your timeline for scaling this?"

The man perked up again, his voice steadier this time. "We've launched trials across several major university campuses: Houston, Austin, Atlanta, and the northeast. College-aged demographics are our initial focus. We're offering a one-week free access pass to generate organic buzz, and we've seen thousands of sign-ups in just days."

Sasha leaned in slightly. "And the engagement rate has surpassed projections. People aren't just signing up, they're staying. They're making meaningful connections. We're changing the dating landscape."

Eric let the silence stretch. He wasn't going to give them more than that just yet.

Barry finally leaned forward, chair legs landing softly on the hardwood. "You said AI. Who built it?" he asked, voice low and even.

Sasha turned toward him, her expression unreadable. "Our in-house team. Three of them are former DARPA contractors. One was lead architect for a behavioral forecasting firm. We own the code outright."

Barry gave a small nod, but his eyes stayed locked on hers a moment longer than polite.

Eric broke the tension with a clipped question. "And what do you want from me? Just money? Or the Whiff name behind your brand?"

Sasha's smile didn't reach her eyes. "Both. But more than that, we want a partner who understands what it means to disrupt expectations."

That got a reaction, not from Eric, but from Barry, who let out a low whistle.

"Careful," he said. "Around here, disruption is the baseline. You'll have to aim higher than that."

After the meeting ended and the presenters left, the heavy glass door clicked shut behind them. Barry waited a beat, then followed Eric down the hall to his office, where the mood was already shifting.

Eric dropped into the leather chair behind his dark walnut desk with a sigh, yanking his tie loose with one hand. The polished office, filled with expensive art and panoramic views of the Houston skyline, suddenly felt too still, too quiet.

"So?" Barry asked, stepping in and letting the door close behind him. He remained standing, hands in his pockets, studying Eric with a cool expression. "What do you think?"

Eric reached for the bottle of sparkling water he'd ignored during the meeting and twisted off the cap. "I think they're ambitious," he said, taking a long sip before setting it down with a soft thunk. "But I don't know if the world needs another dating app."

Barry smirked, finally moving to sit across from him. "Maybe not. But you do."

Eric's brow furrowed as he sat up straighter. "What's that supposed to mean? I'm already dating someone. Crystal."

"It means," Barry said evenly, leaning back with one ankle crossing over his knee, "you've tried finding love the usual way. So how's that working out for you?" He shrugged slightly. "I've been working with you for a week, and I've seen her once. A blurry FaceTime and some high-maintenance texts don't count."

Eric's lips tightened. "She's on that girls' trip to Cabo. She needed a break."

Barry gave a dry chuckle. "Yeah? From what—shopping? Scheduling facials?"

Eric rolled his eyes. "You're suggesting I sign up for a dating app? Are you serious?"

"Why not?" Barry replied, unfazed. "No one has to know. Not even Crystal. We'll set up a profile using a fake name, generic photo, and see what happens. Worst case—you hate it, we delete the account and never speak of it again."

Eric leaned back in his chair, arms crossed, expression skeptical but not dismissive. "You're insane."

Barry shrugged. "And you're bored. Admit it."

Just then, a familiar buzz rattled across the surface of Eric's desk. Again. His phone, face-up and glowing, displayed the name he'd been ignoring for the last hour.

Barry glanced toward it, then back to Eric. "Your phone is buzzing again.

Is it an emergency?"

Eric sighed, rubbing a hand over his jaw. "It's Crystal. Again. She knows I'm in meetings, so why is she calling so much?"

"She knows you're working," Barry said, his tone shifting subtly. "But she's blowing up your phone like it's a crisis. Gut says this isn't good. The day's done. See what she wants."

Eric hesitated, then finally reached for the phone. He didn't call her back immediately. Instead, his thumb slid across the screen, opening his notifications and stopped.

Barry watched his friend's entire demeanor shift.

"What is it?" Barry asked, voice low.

Eric didn't answer right away. He just stared, jaw clenched, as a flush crept up his neck. Then he turned the phone slightly toward Barry.

There it was: an Instagram story, still active and public. Crystal, poolside in Cabo, laughing in a bikini, one arm draped possessively over the shoulders of a sun-kissed man with dark curls and a chiseled jaw. The caption in glitzy script read: *"Best trip ever with my love, Marco! #CaboNights"*.

Barry blinked. "Oof."

Eric's voice was clipped, dark. "She accidentally tagged me in it."

Barry let out a low whistle. "That's… impressively dumb."

Crystal's name flashed across the screen again—an incoming call. Eric hit 'Decline.' It rang again. Another 'Decline.' Then a text appeared: *Eric, baby, it's not what it looks like! Call me! Please!*

Eric stared at it for a moment. Then, with deliberate calm, he answered.

"Save it, Crystal. I saw the post. Have fun in Cabo," he said, his voice so cold it could freeze fire. "And don't bother coming back."

With a sharp flick of his finger, he ended the call and dropped the phone onto the desk. It landed with a hollow, final thud that echoed off the walls.

Silence.

Barry gave it a respectful second, then leaned back, hands behind his head.

"Trouble in paradise?"

Eric ran a hand through his hair, then let it fall limp at his side. "More like a damn hurricane."

Barry grinned. "Well, lucky for you… I just happen to be a survival expert." He stood and reached for the laptop on the corner of the desk. "Let's set up that profile. No time like the present."

Eric gave him a withering look, but the tension in his jaw softened—just a little.

"You're relentless."

Barry smiled, already typing. "You're welcome."

* * *

Barry stood behind Eric's couch, arms crossed, watching in growing disbelief as he swiped through his TruePair matches like a man on a mission.

"No. No. Definitely not. Ehh… nope."

Eric barely gave each profile a second glance before dismissing them with a quick flick of his finger on the tablet.

Barry leaned forward. "You know this isn't a clearance sale, right? You're supposed to read the profiles."

Eric waved him off. "I can tell within three seconds if I'm interested. It's like flipping through a catalog."

Barry exhaled. "A catalog? You're supposed to be looking for a meaningful connection, not picking out furniture."

Eric smirked. "Hey, I'm investing in quality."

Barry groaned. "Are you really? Because you just rejected someone because, and I quote, 'Her earrings were too big.'"

Eric shrugged. "They were too big. They were practically weapons."

Barry let out a dramatic sigh, then, in his usual way, muttered under his breath:

"Shall I compare thee to a summer's day? Nay, your earrings are far too large, I say."

Eric rolled his eyes. "You're impossible."

Barry crossed his arms. "And you're a menace. Have you even read a single profile?"

"I don't need to," Eric said confidently. "You can tell a lot just from pictures."

Barry snatched the tablet out of Eric's hands. "Oh really? Let's test that theory." He scrolled back up to a woman Eric had rejected and read aloud:

"'Maya, 32, pediatric surgeon, volunteers at animal shelters, loves hiking and cooking.'" Barry looked up. "Sounds like a great match."

Eric made a face. "Yeah, but in her second photo, she was holding a parrot."

Barry blinked. "And?"

Eric pointed at the screen. "A parrot, Barry. Do you know how long those things live? That's a lifetime commitment right there. I'm not ready for that kind of responsibility."

Barry stared at him. "You run a billion-dollar company."

Eric took back the tablet. "And that's exactly why I don't need the added stress of a bird."

Barry shook his head, then, with a deadpan expression, recited:

"Love is not love which alters when alteration finds,

Nor is it a parrot, which squawks for all time."

Eric laughed, "I swear, one day I'm going to hire someone to follow you around and write down all this nonsense."

Barry smirked. "You'd have to pay them extra. Genius isn't cheap."

Eric continued swiping. "No. No. Oof, no."

Barry glanced over his shoulder at the latest rejection. "What was wrong with her?"

Eric snorted. "She had a cat named Winston. That's a butler's name."

Barry let out a slow, measured breath. "Eric."

"What?" Eric said defensively. "You wouldn't date someone whose pet had a butler name either."

Barry rubbed his temples, then muttered:

"Of all sad words of tongue or pen,

the saddest are these: she had a cat named Winston."

Eric choked on a laugh. "That is not how that poem goes."

"Close enough," Barry said, reclaiming the tablet. "Now, stop speed-running love and actually read something."

Eric rolled his eyes but humored him, scrolling more slowly. He finally paused at a profile. "Alright, here's one: 'Emma Green, 31, librarian, enjoys classic literature, museums, and coffee shops.'"

Barry perked up. "See? That sounds promising."

Eric studied the profile picture, a woman under an umbrella, her face partially obscured. "Mysterious."

Barry smirked. "Afraid she has a parrot?"

Eric shot him a look. "I'm reading, aren't I?"

Barry crossed his arms. "Good. Because if I see you reject another person because of earrings or butler-named cats, I will revoke your Wi-Fi privileges."

Eric chuckled. "Duly noted."

Barry leaned back with a satisfied sigh and muttered one last time:

"Let us go then, you and I,

and for the love of God, just give someone a try."

Eric laughed, shaking his head. Maybe, just maybe, he'd take Barry's advice this time.

Chapter 4

Claire

Claire sat at her desk in the Perry Library, the familiar scent of old books and lemon-scented floor polish grounding her in the present, even as her mind wandered. Her turkey sandwich remained wrapped in wax paper beside a sweating can of Diet Coke, both untouched.

The afternoon sun filtered through the tall windows, casting a pale grid across the floor and climbing the legs of her desk like a net trying to catch her.

She stared at her open laptop, TruePair glowing brightly in front of her. It had been two days since she signed up: two days of avoidance, second-guessing, and wondering what exactly she thought she was doing.

It wasn't for lack of matches. The app was relentless. Each morning it chimed cheerfully:

"Emma, we've found someone who might truly understand you!"

The message made her cringe every time. Emma. She still wasn't used to it. The name felt like a borrowed coat—familiar in function, but stiff in the sleeves and not quite hers. She'd chosen it for a reason: it was safe, unsearchable, and forgettable. Less intimate than Claire. Less vulnerable.

She tapped her pen against the corner of her notebook, the rhythmic clicking lost beneath the ambient hum of the library's fluorescent lights and the occasional echo of a student coughing or a book being reshelved.

The cursor blinked patiently. She minimized the TruePair tab, tried to focus on the JSTOR article she'd queued up that morning: *"The Impact of 19th Century Women regarding a 21st Century Literary Landscape."* Normally, the topic would've held her attention—how women dealt with literature on a civic level, how the 1800s wove itself into today's infrastructure. But today, the words on the screen blurred into static.

With a sigh, she toggled back to the TruePair tab.

Maybe just one look.

Click.

A grid of profile photos loaded. Her breath caught slightly, not in anticipation, but in the sort of dread that came with opening an old journal or stepping onto an unfamiliar stage.

There they were: a mosaic of strangers. Some smiled too hard. Some didn't smile at all. A few looked like they were still in college. One wore a tank top and flexed at the gym mirror. Another held a trout like it was a passport. One had written, *"Looking for someone who can handle the real me. No drama."*

Claire scoffed softly. Translation: all drama.

And then she saw one.

No photo. Just a minimalist profile picture—a gray silhouette, like a default setting. Username: **Ethan Wells**.

No flashy tagline. Just two sentences in the bio section:

"Business owner. Learning to be more open, one word at a time."

She frowned. Something about that felt… deliberate. Measured. Maybe even… careful.

Her finger hovered over the profile. For once, her instinct wasn't immediate dismissal.

Still, she couldn't bring herself to click on any.

"Lost in thought, or just avoiding work?"

Claire looked up, startled. Muriel stood in the doorway, one brow arched high and her hair falling in a smooth, straight bob, the sharp edges grazing her jawline. Her gold hoop earrings swinging with purpose. She wore a bold red dress, sandals, and carried a smoothie filled with something that looked suspiciously like kale blended with regret.

Claire closed the laptop like it was evidence. "Neither. Lunch break."

Muriel took one slow step into the office, eyes narrowing like she was about to lay hands. "Mmm. That was a *guilty* laptop slam. What were you doing? Watching baby goats in pajamas? Online stalking your ex's new girlfriend?"

Claire sighed. "Fine. I signed up for a dating app. TruePair."

Muriel froze. Then, slowly, she lowered herself into the chair across from Claire. "Say what?"

Claire groaned. "I said I signed up for TruePair."

Muriel's face broke into a grin so wide it could part clouds. "Thank you, Jesus! I've hoped you would do something ever since Sam the Damp Washcloth walked out of your life and sucked the flavor right out of your soul."

"I dumped Sam."

"You *gracefully* released him into the wild like he was a rescued squirrel. I was ready to kick him out on your behalf."

Claire snorted. "You know, some people might think that's extreme."

"Some people aren't your best friend," Muriel shot back. "I saw you pouring out, girl, and Sam was sipping with a cracked cup."

Claire stared at her, then slowly grinned. "Okay, that was good."

Muriel took a triumphant sip of her smoothie. "Don't act surprised. I'm sassy and still got common sense. Now—tell me you used a fake name. Please tell me you didn't put 'Claire the Librarian' with a sunflower emoji."

"I used Emma."

Muriel nodded, satisfied. "Emma. That's safe. Sounds like she composts, but also makes a mean lemon pound cake for the church bake sale. I like her."

Claire chuckled. "I wanted to keep it impersonal."

"Well, Emma better find a man who can spell 'boundaries' and doesn't list 'vibes' as his religion." Muriel leaned in. "So. Any contenders?"

Claire hesitated. "One, maybe. No photo. Just a name—Ethan Wells—and a short bio. Says he's a business owner, learning to be more open, one word at a time."

Muriel tilted her head. "Huh. That's either really deep or he's in therapy and hasn't told his mama yet." She reached for the laptop and peered at the profile. "Okay, I'll give him this, he didn't say 'no drama,' which usually means *all* the drama."

Claire exhaled. "Yeah I remembered you telling me that. I skipped over another guy because of it. I haven't messaged this one yet."

Muriel leaned back, giving Claire the full church-mother look—half love, half challenge. "You keep asking for something different, but when it shows up, you sit there like it's a math test. Message the man, Claire."

Claire gave her a look. "You really think he's different?"

"I think," Muriel said, standing up, "that sometimes *you* have to make the first move. Faith without works is dead, remember?"

Claire rolled her eyes affectionately. "You're matchmaking now?"

Muriel grinned, hand on the door. "I'm a multi-talented person. Now send that message. And if he turns out to be crazy, I got a cousin who used to box."

Claire looked at his profile again, cursor hovering over the button.

His profile picture was simple, black and white, slightly angled, not flashy, but a little grainy. A man with short, light-colored hair, sharp eyes, and a confident smile. He looked decent but not immediately recognizable.

Claire's finger hovered one last time.

And then—click.

She did it.

She sat back in her chair, heartbeat steadying, her breath slowing.

Claire exhaled. "Okay. One match checked."

Muriel broke into a grin that was ninety percent pride and ten percent *finally*. "How does Ethan measure up from the Land of the Faceless?"

Claire tilted her head, uncertain. "I don't know. He seems… normal? Thoughtful, maybe."

Muriel crossed her arms. "So not a crypto bro, a bass fisherman, or someone looking for a 'Disney princess who can hang with the guys'? That's a win."

Claire gave her a side glance. "It's just one profile."

Muriel leaned on the desk. "Girl, that's all it takes."

Claire laughed despite herself. "Let's not compare Ethan Wells to the rest yet."

Muriel chuckled. "Fine, but let's not let it sit there, either. You swiped. Good. Now *message* him. Let's get this faith train moving."

Claire hesitated, staring at the blank message box. "Maybe I should wait. See if he writes first."

Muriel's eyes widened. "Claire Noelle Eidean. You clicked. That was the first act of bravery. Now show me you're the woman I know you are—the one who can run a fundraising event with one hand and shut down a faculty budget meeting with the other."

Claire gave a reluctant smile. "Alright, alright. I'll message him."

Muriel clapped her hands once, loud enough to startle a student in the hallway. "That's my girl! We are making progress today!"

Claire shook her head, grinning. "You're really enjoying this."

"Oh, I live for this," Muriel said. "Now don't overthink it. Say something smart. Say something real. And if he turns out to be a fool, I'll send you memes to get you through."

Claire shook her head, fingers hovering over the keyboard.

Emma*: So do you think TruePair works, or did we both just fall for good marketing?*

She hit SEND before second-guessing herself.

Muriel waggled her eyebrows. "See? That wasn't so bad."

Claire shut her laptop. "We'll see."

For the first time in a long time, she felt something strange.

Possibility.

Muriel leaned back in her chair. "By the way, I saw what you ordered this morning. Another iced brown sugar oat milk espresso with salted caramel foam? You're such a librarian stereotype."

Claire scoffed. "It's delicious. And sophisticated."

Muriel snickered. "Claire, it's a glorified milkshake. Just like this dating thing, you gotta mix it up sometimes."

* * *

Claire stared at her phone all evening, the soft glow of the screen, the only light in her dimly lit apartment. The message she'd sent to Ethan Wells was still unread.

She frowned. Maybe this was a mistake.

She had no reason to be nervous, after all, it wasn't her putting herself out there. It was Emma Green, a carefully curated version. Still, waiting for a response felt oddly personal.

Claire sighed and set the phone down. Whatever happens, happens.

She got up to make a cup of tea, needing something warm to settle her nerves. The electric kettle hummed to life on the counter in the kitchen as she reached for her favorite oversized mug—the one with a chipped rim and faded quote from *Little Women*.

Steam curled into the air, and for a brief moment, the world felt normal again.

Then a sharp *ding* shattered the quiet.

Her phone.

The sound sliced through the stillness like a firecracker, and Claire jumped. Her elbow bumped the edge of the counter, and in her startled scramble to grab the phone, it slipped from her grasp, pinged off the corner of her chair, ricocheted against the wall—and slid with a faint *skritch* under the dresser.

Claire groaned, pushing herself up to retrieve it. As she bent down, her cat, Oliver, padded over, tail twitching with curiosity, peered under the dresser beside her, hoping she'd pull out one of his forgotten toys. She jumped, her heart leaping into her throat. A message.

Ethan: *Well, if we're both here, then either it works... or we're both terrible at dating.*

Claire blinked at the response. Not bad. She typed back.

Emma: *I was hoping it wasn't the latter. But I suppose time will tell.*

A response came almost immediately.

Ethan: *Tell me, Emma Green, what made you give this thing a shot? Are you a* *believer in science and algorithms? Or just looking for a good story?*

Claire hesitated before responding.

Emma: *A little of both. And you?*

Ethan: *I'm here because a friend convinced me. I have a bad habit of judging people before I know them.*

Claire tilted her head. That was… an interesting admission.

Emma: *That's an honest answer. Most people would say something more charming.*

Ethan: *I saved the charm for later. Gotta keep some mystery alive.*

Claire laughed softly to herself.

Emma: *Ah, so you admit to using charm as a strategy.*

Ethan: *It's a necessary skill in my line of work.*

Claire narrowed her eyes.

Emma: *And what is that, exactly?*

A pause. Then,

Ethan: *Business. Negotiations. Making things happen.*

Claire rolled her eyes. Vague. And suspicious.

Emma: *That sounds like the bio of a man who enjoys expensive suits and making deals over whiskey.*

Ethan: *You're not entirely wrong.*

Of course she wasn't.

Emma: *And yet you're here on a dating app. Looking for something algorithms claim to be able to find.*

Ethan: *What can I say? Even people in suits like a good mystery.*

Claire tapped her fingers against the edge of her phone, contemplating. He was clever, but he wasn't over-the-top. He didn't try to impress her, just conversing.

And somehow, it was easier.

Emma: *Fine. We'll see if this thing works. However I should warn you, I don't believe in perfect matches.*

Ethan: *Good. Then we have something in common.*

Claire stared at the screen for a moment longer, placed her phone face down on the table, then slowly exhaled.

This was a terrible idea.

And yet...

* * *

Her phone buzzed, but this time it wasn't TruePair. She glanced at the screen and frowned. A message from an unknown number.

Unknown: *"Hey, Claire. It's me. Don't freak out."*

Her breath hitched. Only one person sent such messages.

Chloe.

Her elusive baby sister.

Claire sat up straighter, her fingers ready to text back. It wasn't long since she last heard from Chloe, but every message felt like a rare occurrence.

Claire: *"Chloe? Where are you?"*

The texting bubbles appeared, then disappeared. Claire's stomach twisted. Finally, a reply.

Chloe: *"I can't say. But I need your help. Can we talk?"*

A sharp pang shot through Claire's chest. She spent months respecting Chloe's privacy since her sister didn't want to be found. And now, when Claire started focusing on her own life again, Chloe reappeared with a cryptic message?

She clenched her jaw, typing back.

Claire: *"Of course. Call me. Now."*

A long pause. Then,

Chloe: *"I can't. Not yet. But soon. Promise."*

Claire exhaled, frustration and relief tangling inside her.

She leaned back against the couch, absentmindedly running her fingers through Oliver's soft fur as he settled beside her. His rhythmic purring filled the quiet room, a soothing hum against her shattered thoughts. Claire let her eyes drift closed, remembering the past.

There was a time when their family felt whole. When all three sisters were under the same roof, their mother was bustling around and keeping everything together. After their father passed, Claire believed they would stay strong, bound together by grief and love. But today told a different story, one of distance, avoidance, and broken trust.

Oliver nuzzled into her palm, sensing her sadness. She let out a slow breath, brushing a hand over his head. Maybe Chloe reaching out was the first step toward mending what was lost. Despite the past, if Claire wanted a future, then she couldn't live there.

Chapter 5

Eric

The Railway Interchange Conference was the place where Eric thrived with its glimmering chandeliers, polished egos, and bottomless potential. Deals weren't made on paper. Instead, they sparked over handshakes, champagne flutes, and the unspoken competition of who seemed more important. High-speed trains were the future, and Eric wanted to fund them.

With the day done and deals completed, it was time for fun. Eric leaned against the bar, drink in hand, the warm burn of aged bourbon coating his throat. Somewhere behind him, Barry was doing his usual bodyguard hover, arms crossed, eyes scanning the room like they were one step from a heist. The man did not know how to relax.

Eric, on the other hand, was on his third, maybe fourth drink and enjoying the easy flirtation of a woman in a black dress with a neckline that defied gravity. Vanessa? No, Valerie. Whatever her name was, she was practically draped on him, her fingers tracing idle shapes against his chest.

Crystal was long gone, on to her next opportunity, just like he'd expected. No texts. No drama. Just another polished goodbye in his long line of beautiful, forgettable exits. He wasn't looking for commitment tonight just distraction. And Valerie, or whatever, was exactly that.

She laughed at something he said, maybe about bullet trains or the absurdity of Texas real estate, he honestly didn't remember, and leaned in close enough for her perfume to fill his senses.

He noticed Barry walking in his direction as Valerie ran her hand lower and met his gaze.

"This is Barry," Eric told her as he waved a hand, grinning. "My very serious bodyguard."

The woman giggled. "A bodyguard? That's so… dangerous."

Barry gave his trademark nod, tight-lipped, unimpressed.

Eric rolled his eyes. "Come on, Barry. We're celebrating. Progress, innovation, the future!"

Barry looked at the woman, then back at Eric. "And what's she celebrating?"

Valerie pouted, almost convincingly. "I just love brilliant minds. Men who build things…"

Eric let her keep talking. It didn't matter if she meant it. It was nice to be admired, for something other than his bank account, even if that admiration came with glittering false lashes and suspicious timing.

When she suggested his hotel room, because why not?, Barry's tone changed instantly. "Eric."

Not again.

Eric groaned. "Don't start."

"I'm serious," Barry warned. "You go off alone with her, I can't protect you."

Eric smirked. "I don't need protecting from her."

Barry's sigh was theatrical, followed by one of his poems:
"A fool and his judgment part ways in the night,
Led by a siren, lost to the light."

Eric rolled his eyes. "Come on, Barry. Can I live a little?"

The woman clung tighter to his arm, smiling with glossy lips. "Eric's a big boy," she purred. "He can make his own choices."

"Terrible ones," Barry muttered under his breath.

Eric shot Barry a look. "That's why I keep you around."

As they stepped into the elevator, Eric didn't look back.

Later, Eric lay awake, the city glowing beneath the tall windows, while Valerie padded around in one of his shirts, her voice suddenly different, less breathy, more calculated.

"Do you keep the minibar stocked with the imported stuff? Or should I just call room service?"

Eric blinked. "Uh, yeah. Help yourself."

She hummed, already pulling bottles from the fridge. "You ever think about investing in nightlife? I know a guy who's opening a new club in Miami. With your kind of money, it'd be a breeze."

He frowned slightly. "I usually stick to infrastructure."

She turned, drink in hand, and perched on the edge of the bed like she belonged there. "Infrastructure's sexy if it gets you into the right circles. But if you want visibility, you gotta be where the celebrities are."

Eric sat up. The air between them felt different now. Heavy. He wasn't interested in fame full-time. He didn't like the attention he'd received from the media now.

"I think I'm okay with staying under the radar," he said slowly.

Valerie shrugged. "Suit yourself. But those who stay invisible usually get left behind."

Eric watched her sip the expensive liquor like it was water. Suddenly, the warmth of the evening felt cheap. Transactional. She wasn't here for charm or intellect, just opportunity. They all were. Only this time it bothered him.

"I've got a meeting early," he said, sliding from the bed. and heading to the bathroom.

"Of course you do," she said, not bothering to hide the sarcasm.

"You need to go. I have cash on the desk for your time." He told her as he turned on the shower.

Barry was right.

Again.

* * *

Eric Whiff squinted against the morning sun as he stumbled out of the Grand Meridian Hotel, each step a betrayal of the night before. His head throbbed, his suit was a rumpled wreck, and his mouth tasted like regret chased with champagne.

He spotted Barry's black SUV idling at the curb like a judgmental shadow. Of course, he was here. Always watching.

"Good morning," Barry rolled down the window.

Eric pulled open the passenger door and slid in with a groan. "Not so loud," he muttered.

Barry didn't miss a beat. "Oh, I'm whispering. This is my inside voice."

Eric winced as the vehicle pulled away. He slouched in the seat, shielding his eyes. "You look like a man who's made a series of regrettable choices," Barry added.

Eric offered a faint smile. "That depends on how we define 'regrettable.'"

Barry's voice took on an edge. "Do you remember anything from last night?"

"Vaguely," Eric admitted. He wasn't proud of it. Vanessa, Valerie? Veronica? She looked dazzling in the bar's low light, but the glitter didn't hold up in the morning.

"She lost interest the moment I stopped ordering champagne by the bottle," he confessed, rubbing his temple.

Barry shook his head. "Classic gold-digger with a short attention span."

Eric exhaled. "I should've listened to you."

"Yes, you should've," Barry said. "So now, tell me, what's missing?"

Eric blinked. "Missing?

"Your wallet? Your watch? Your dignity?"

Eric gave himself a quick pat-down. "I sent her away early. Paid her well. Wallet's here. Rolex watch is… not. It was my dad's."

Barry reached into the glove compartment and tossed the antique watch onto Eric's lap. "I tailed her after she left. Took it back before she disappeared with it. Didn't break her wrist, either. You're welcome."

Eric stared at the watch in surprise. "You're the best, Barry."

Barry's voice was weary. "No. I'm just tired."

Then, in that poetic monotone of his, he murmured:
"Fools chase pleasure, heedless and blind,
Only to wake with regret on their mind."
Eric groaned. "Seriously with the poetry?"
"If you listened, you wouldn't wake up like a budget crime scene."
Eric chuckled despite himself, then grew quiet. "Okay, okay. No more Valeries."
Barry didn't let up. "You are saying that now, or do you mean it?"
"I mean it," Eric said. And he did. For once, the night's mistakes left more than just embarrassment, they left him hollow. "I think I need to change. I can't let people in who only see the bank account."
Barry gave him a rare approving nod. "Now that's the first intelligent thing you've said in weeks."
Eric glanced out the window. "So what now? Enlighten me, O Brooding One."
Barry smirked. "Lucky for you, you signed up for TruePair. Try reading the profiles instead of dismissing people because of their earrings."
Eric groaned. "That was one time."
"One time too many," Barry shot back. "Next time I'm charging you extra to chase down stolen accessories."
Eric laughed. "Duly noted."
The SUV rolled forward, Houston's skyline sparkling in the distance. For once, the silence between them wasn't awkward, it was thoughtful.
Maybe Barry was right. Maybe this time could be different.
Maybe, just maybe, he was finally tired of being the fool.

* * *

Eric sat on the plush couch in his penthouse, phone in hand, fixated on the blinking cursor in his TruePair chat. Normally, he was decisive about sealing a business deal, negotiating a merger, or engaging in casual flirtation. Now crafting a simple message felt unnerving.

He glanced up at Barry, who lounged in the armchair across from him, arms folded and amusement dancing in his eyes.

"Well?" Barry prodded. "What's holding you up? You've been staring at that screen for five minutes."

Eric sighed, scrolling over Emma's latest message.

Emma: *Fine. We'll see if this thing works. But I should warn you, I don't believe in perfect matches.*

"I don't want to come off too eager," Eric admitted, his tone uncertain.

Barry raised an eyebrow. "Eager is your middle name, isn't it?"

"Yeah, but don't advertise it," Eric muttered, rereading the message as if it held the secret to his future.

Barry leaned towards Eric with a playful glint. "In that case, let me lend you some of my charm. You need something captivating and witty, right?"

Eric managed a half-smile. "Exactly. Help me out, will you?

After Barry's thoughtful pause, "Write this down: 'Perfection is boring anyway. I prefer something with a little mystery.'"

Eric typed the words and read them aloud softly. "Not bad."

Barry snorted. "High praise, coming from a guy who judged a woman over her earrings."

Ignoring the jab, Eric hit send. Almost immediately, the typing indicator flickered on the screen.

Emma: *Good answer. Mystery makes things interesting. But tell me, what's the last thing that truly surprised you?*

Eric hesitated, his fingers hovering over the keyboard. "Okay… now what?"

Barry smirked. "Whatever you do, don't say 'the stock market.'"

Eric scoffed. "I wasn't going to say that," he replied, then paused. "But hypothetically, that would be surprising, "

"No," Barry interrupted firmly. "Pick something human."

After a moment's thought, Eric slowly typed:

Eric: *A woman who reads my messages and challenges me. That's rare.*

Barry leaned over and nodded. "Alright, I'll allow that one."

Moments later, another message appeared on the screen.

Emma: *Points for honesty. I'll admit, I like challenges too.*

A genuine grin tugged at Eric's lips. "I think I'm doing pretty well."

Barry gave him a flat look. "We are doing well. You'd be three bad metaphors deep by now if I wasn't here to steer you."

Eric chuckled and set his phone aside. "You know, Barry, for a guy who quotes poetry about fools, you're decent at this."

Barry leaned back with a half-smile. "Let's just say I have more faith in words than in you."

"Then keep that faith, my friend," Eric grinned. "Because I think this one might be worth it."

Barry's smirk deepened. "We'll see."

For the first time in a while, Eric felt a spark of genuine curiosity, this job wasn't just another fleeting chase. Something real might be on the horizon, hidden behind the mystery and honesty of a single, well-chosen phrase.

* * *

Eric sat at his kitchen bar; his eyes fixed on the TruePair chat with Emma Green. There was something about talking to her that had captivated him. Emma was sharp and witty, nothing like the women he usually encountered. No lavish flirtations, no veiled mentions of money. Just genuine, engaging conversation. And that, Eric mused, was what made him suspicious.

He began scrolling through her profile again. It was as enigmatic as it was sparse: a self-described librarian who adored books and coffee, with a penchant for mystery. Her profile picture offered only a partial glimpse of her beneath an umbrella, a deliberately subtle reveal. Too perfect, in a way that made Eric's gut twist.

"What if she's not real?" he muttered under his breath.

Barry looked up from his phone as he walked into the room. "What?"

Eric's voice grew low as he outlined his growing concern. "What if she's a journalist trying to get a story on me? Or worse, some kind of stalker?"

Barry arched an eyebrow. "You realize how paranoid you sound, right?"

Eric didn't laugh.

Barry leaned back in his chair, crossing his arms. "Look, I built your profile myself, remember? No photos linked to your real name. No mention of Whiff Industries, your job, or anything else that could connect the dots. The only way she'd know who you are is if you told her."

Eric ran a hand through his hair. "Still… something feels off."

Barry sighed. "Then stop messaging her."

Eric looked at him like he'd suggested canceling electricity. "I can't. Not yet."

Barry studied him for a beat. "You like her."

"I don't even know her," Eric muttered.

Barry smirked. "That's not what your face says."

Eric frowned, frustration creeping in. "Barry, every woman I've met in the last five years has had an angle. What are the odds that this is the one genuine person?"

Barry let out a resigned sigh. "Considering you've chosen women for their Instagram aesthetics; I'd say the odds are pretty low."

Eric shot him a look that blended exasperation and determination. "Exactly my point. I can't trust this until I know who she is." Leaning forward, he added, "Find out for me."

Barry blinked in disbelief. "You're serious? You just started texting her yesterday. Are you falling that quickly?"

"Dead serious. Besides, the week of free service ends any day now. What if she decides not to sign up?" Eric replied, his tone leaving no room for doubt.

Barry rubbed his temples and exhaled slowly. "So, let me get this straight. You meet a woman who isn't out to bankrupt you, and your first instinct is to have me investigate her background?"

Eric nodded, his eyes narrowing slightly.

Barry let out a long, slow whistle. "Wow. Therapy is really going to love you."

Eric rolled his eyes. "I'm being smart this time, not paranoid."

Barry leaned back with a wry smile. "Smart? Or just crazy?"

"Call it whatever you want," Eric shrugged, "but I need to be sure."

After a long moment of study, Barry shook his head. "Fine. I'll investigate her. But just so we're clear, if she turns out to be a normal person who likes you for you, I am never letting you live this down."

A smirk tugged at Eric's lips. "Deal."

Barry muttered under his breath,

"The fool who doubts the gift of fate,

May find his truth a moment too late."

Eric grinned. "You should really write those down."

Barry sighed as he began pulling up his contacts. "Oh, don't worry. One day, when you ruin your own happiness, I will."

Eric narrowed his eyes. Barry's fingers moved quickly over his phone; his expression unreadable, focused, tight.

"Who are you texting?" Eric asked, watching him.

Barry didn't look up. "Someone who owes me a favor."

Eric's jaw tensed. "Barry."

Still no eye contact. "Relax. Just getting eyes in a few places. You want me to find out who she is or not?"

Chapter 6

Claire

Claire tapped her fingers against the keyboard, but her attention refused to settle on the rhythm of academic journals and research requests. Her thoughts drifted to the chat, back to him.

She hadn't expected to enjoy texting Ethan Wells on TruePair. But she did. More than she wanted to admit. His messages were clever and curious. The conversation felt easy, unforced. No awkward small talk. No pressure to impress.

It was refreshing. Intoxicating, even.

For once, she wasn't the overworked librarian or the responsible sister. She was *Emma Green*, witty, curious, untethered, trading barbs with someone who made her grin at her phone like a teenager.

And yet? Something didn't sit right.

If she was going to keep this going, she had to decide soon. Her free trial on TruePair expired in a day.

There were no red flags. No invasive questions. No smarmy compliments that made her cringe. On the surface, Ethan Wells was ideal, smart, funny and engaging.

But a quiet voice in the back of her mind whispered: *Something's off.*

Not loud. Not dramatic. Just… persistent.

The kind of whisper that didn't go away.

Maybe it was guilt gnawing at her, because she wasn't being honest either. *Emma Green* didn't exist. She'd made sure of that. So, who was to say *Ethan Wells* was any different?

Claire leaned back into her chair, exhaling slowly as the thought that had been circling her mind like a vulture finally landed.

I could look him up.

The idea came so naturally and it startled her. It was what she did. Before the library, before academia, she'd spent years at a law firm combing through public records piecing together timelines, uncovering the truths people thought were safely buried.

Her fingers hovered above the keyboard.

Would it be wrong?

It wouldn't take much. A few keystrokes, maybe a reverse image search. She could know, *really* know, who he was in minutes.

But the real question pressed harder than the ethical one:

Did she want to know?

The unease twisting in her gut battled with her curiosity. What was she hoping to find? A reason to walk away? A red flag to validate the instinct she couldn't quite explain?

Or, worse, proof that he was exactly who he claimed to be.

With a steady breath, she typed his name.

Ethan Wells. Houston, Texas.

Nothing.

Claire frowned. That was unexpected.

Even the most private people left behind a trail, a LinkedIn profile, a public record, an old class roster, maybe even a half-forgotten Myspace page buried in the digital graveyard.

But this?

This was a ghost.

She refined her search, added parameters, toggled filters, tried alternate spellings, but still nothing.

Her heart ticked faster.

Either he was incredibly private or he wasn't real.

A chill slid down her spine, not quite fear, but something close. The feeling she got when pieces didn't fit. A mystery. A challenge. A puzzle begging to be solved.

She leaned back her eyes fixed on the empty search results.

So, he's lying about his name.

She should've felt that familiar prickle of wariness that always came with deception.

Instead, her lips curved.

Because honestly, who was she to judge? *Emma Green* was no more real than *Ethan Wells*.

She ran her tongue along her teeth, a quiet laugh catching in her throat.

"Well, well, Mr. Wells," she murmured. "Looks like we're both playing pretend."

And now, there was only one question left:

Who would uncover the truth first?

* * *

Claire shut her laptop with a quiet *click*, the glow of the screen vanishing, but the questions it stirred remained. Her search for *Ethan Wells* had turned up nothing, and that was a problem. A man like him, sharp, articulate, intriguing, should have left a digital footprint even a faint one.

She wasn't sure if that should worry her or amuse her.

Her fingers traced the edge of her coffee cup, *iced brown sugar oat milk espresso with salted caramel foam.* Her one indulgence, the only luxury she allowed herself in a life where she was always the responsible one. Always practical. Always the one expected to fix things.

Just as she lifted the cup to take a sip, her phone vibrated against the desk, rattling her nerves. She glanced at the screen.

Camila.

Claire sighed and let it ring once more before finally answering. "Hey, Camila."

"Finally," her sister huffed. "I was about to call the library and have them page you."

Claire resisted the urge to roll her eyes. "What's up?"

"I need you to pick up Mom's new medication on your way over."

She blinked. "What?"

"You are coming over tonight, right?"

Claire had planned to stop by later in the week, but apparently, Camila had other ideas.

"I, "

"Claire, come on. I barely got any sleep last night. Mom had a bad night, and Charles must rent a car to go to the BoldlyGo Expo in Atlanta. We have to get the car." Camila's voice lowered to a sharp whisper. "The twins are running me ragged, and Mom, she's just getting worse. I need a break. You're single and you don't have anything else to do."

Guilt hit Claire like a stone sinking in water. She could picture it now, her mother slumped in her recliner, hands trembling as she struggled to lift a glass of water. Camila pacing, snapping at Charles while the kids screamed in the background.

She gripped her coffee cup tighter. "I'll be there," she said quietly.

"Great. And don't forget the prescription."

The line went dead.

Claire exhaled, setting her phone down with a little too much force. She knew she *shouldn't* feel irritated. Camila was carrying the heavier burden, living in the house, dealing with the day-to-day chaos. But sometimes, it felt like Claire was expected to be the backup generator, only called upon when things went dark. Then, where was Chloe in times like these? Her baby sister with the mysterious texts but never calling.

She took a long sip of her coffee, closing her eyes as the sweet, salty foam melted on her tongue.

It was always the same. The same obligations. The same expectations. The same guilt.

And yet, the one thing that made her feel *different*, the one thing that pulled her out of her usual routine lately, was Ethan Wells, who didn't even exist.

A bitter laugh slipped past her lips.

She spent all this time unraveling his secret, but maybe it was time to confront her own.

Was she truly looking for love? Or just an escape?

A notification flashed across her phone's screen:

Don't let them get away! TruePair's week of free service expires soon! Sign up now!

* * *

Claire pulled into the driveway of her childhood home, the old brick house standing as a quiet sentinel of memories, some warm, some suffocating. The porch light flickered slightly, and the familiar sag in the front steps reminded her how long since her father was around to fix things.

Before she stepped inside with purse and meds in hand, Camila was at the door, coat on, her expression tight with exhaustion.

"Thank God. We won't be too long," she said, almost jerking Claire inside.

Charles appeared behind her, grinning as he adjusted his Starfleet commander baseball cap. "Kids had an early dinner, and Mom's meds are by her chair. Just make sure she takes them, and, uh, " He glanced toward the living room, where the sounds of gunfire and shouting echoed from a video game. "Maybe check on them every once in a while."

Claire barely had time to respond before Camila and Charles were out the door, the cold night air swallowing their retreat.

Inside, the house was a mixture of familiar scents, something vaguely burned from the kitchen, old furniture, and the ever-present smell of her mother's lavender lotion.

Beatrice Eidean sat in her recliner with a soft blanket draped over her legs. Her body appeared smaller every time Claire saw her, her once sharp eyes dulled by fatigue and medication.

"Hey, Mom," Claire said, settling onto the couch beside her.

Her mother gave a slight smile, more of a small shift in her expression. She no longer spoke much, MS had stolen her words, just as it had stolen her mobility.

"Hello, dear." Beatrice replied but focused on the TV screen.

A black-and-white western playing some old John Wayne film full of slow dialogue and dusty saloons. Claire sighed. *Of course.* It was their dad's favorite and mom loved them.

The kids, Nathan, who was nine, and the twins, Henry and Olivia, both seven, were sprawled on the floor, glued to their game console.

Claire let the minutes stretch allowing herself to slip into the quiet monotony. The occasional hoarse laugh from the TV. The rapid tapping of game controllers. The distant hum of traffic outside.

Her fingers inched toward her phone.

Before she could stop herself, she pulled up her chat with Ethan Wells.

So far, their conversations included light observations and random quirks. Nothing too personal. Nothing that would require peeling back the layers.

But tonight, sitting here in the dim glow of the TV while the weight of expectation pressed down on her, she wanted something more.

Claire: *I have a question for you.*

He replied almost instantly.

Ethan: *Hit me with it.*

She hesitated, then typed:

Claire: *Can you handle the deep emotional stuff?*

The dots appeared. Stopped. Appeared again. Then his answer came through.

Ethan: *Try me.*

Claire swallowed.

She started typing.

Claire: *My mom has MS. She can't do much anymore, and my sister has taken over her care, but she resents me for not being around more. And maybe she's right. Maybe I don't do enough. But every time I come here, I feel like I'm suffocating. And then I feel guilty for feeling that way.*

She stared at the message, debating whether to send it.

Then, before she could overthink it, she pressed send.

Seconds passed.

Then minutes.

The waiting stretched.

Just as she was about to regret opening up, his reply came through.

Ethan: *That sounds hard. You must love your mom a lot. And it sounds like you're carrying more than you let on.*

Claire let out a breath she hadn't realized she was holding.

Ethan: *I don't know if it helps, but... you're allowed to feel overwhelmed. It doesn't mean you love her any less. My mother also died when I was a kid of something similar. My dad and I watched her waste away. It never gets easy.*

Her throat tightened.

Maybe Ethan Wells wasn't real.

But at this moment, he felt like the most real thing in her life.

* * *

Claire stared at the screen, her heart thudding in a slow, heavy rhythm. The words settled deep inside her, pressing against something raw, something she hadn't allowed herself to acknowledge. She swallowed hard, her fingers tightening around her phone.

She wanted to believe him. Wanted to believe that love and exhaustion could coexist, that being here, watching over her mother, stepping in for her sister, drowning in the weight of it all, didn't mean she was failing.

Another message popped up.

Ethan: *Does she still recognize you?*

Claire blinked, caught off guard by the question.

She glanced at her mother, who was staring blankly at the television screen, her frail hands folded in her lap.

Claire: *Yes. I think so. But it's hard to tell sometimes. Just nods or smiles a little. It's like she's still here, but not like it used to be.*

Ethan: *That must be hard. To love someone who's slipping away in slow motion.*

Claire's throat tightened.

Claire: *Yeah. It is.*

She shifted on the couch, glancing toward the kids. The twins were still playing, shouting at the screen in bursts of excitement. Nathan sat farther back, quieter, his brows drawn in frustration.

She looked at the clock. It had been nearly an hour since Camila and Charles left.

Claire: *And then there's my sister. She's the one who takes care of her day in and day out. She means well, but sometimes takes things too far. She acts like I get the easy way out, just swooping in whenever it's convenient.*

The response came quicker this time.

Ethan: *Do you?*

Claire hesitated.

Did she?

Was she the one avoiding the worst of it?

Before she could answer, a loud noise made her jerk her head up.

"I didn't do anything!" Nathan's voice rose, defensive and frustrated.

"You messed up the game!" Henry shot back; his face scrunched in anger.

Claire sighed, rubbing her temples. "Guys, seriously?"

Nathan pushed himself up, crossing his arms. "They're just blaming me because they lost!"

"Because you lost for us!" Olivia snapped.

"Okay, okay," Claire cut in, standing. "It's just a game. Maybe take a break?"

"No!" Henry and Olivia said in unison.

Nathan scoffed. "See?"

Claire groaned. She did not have the energy for this.

She sank back onto the couch, picking up her phone, feeling the exhaustion settle deeper into her bones.

Claire: *Sorry, kid crisis. I swear, being here is like walking into a hurricane.*

Ethan: *Sounds like you need a drink.*

She let out a quiet laugh.

Claire: *Or five.*

Ethan: *Tell me what you'd have, and I'll have one in solidarity.*

She hesitated for a second before smirking.

Claire: *Coffee...a nice cup of coffee. Venti. Cold brew.*

Ethan: *Wow.*

Claire: *What?*

Ethan: *That was... unexpected.*

She laughed, covering her mouth to keep from waking her mom.

Claire: *What were you expecting?*

Ethan: *Whiskey.*

Claire: *I'll save that after I put the kids to bed.*

Ethan: *Fair.*

Claire found herself smiling, the tension in her shoulders loosening just a bit.

Ethan: *For the record, I'd try your cold coffee. But if it's terrible, I reserve the right to mock you mercilessly.*

Claire: *Deal.*

Ethan: *So, is it a date? TruePair expires tomorrow, you know.*

She leaned her head back against the couch, her exhaustion still present but softened at the edges.

Maybe this strange, anonymous connection was what she needed tonight.

Claire: *Yes, yes, it is. There is a coffee shop, called Moody Grounds, next to the University. Have you heard of it? Can you meet me after work on Friday? I will sit in the back facing the window.*

Eric: *Wonderful! See you soon and everything will be fine. You'll see.*

And maybe, just maybe, she wasn't as alone in all of this as she thought.

Chapter 7

Barry

Barry Poet didn't trust auction houses. Too many loafers pretending to be Oxford scholars, all elbow patches and ego, squinting through thin-rimmed glasses as if the spirit of Sotheby's might descend upon them mid-bid. Still, here he was, shoulders hunched in the fifth row of a creaky folding chair, surrounded by the scent of polished mahogany and desperation.

Eric Whiff, on the other hand, was practically vibrating with energy. He twitched like a caffeinated squirrel with a paddle, eyes darting between the catalog and the stage as if they were at a high-stakes poker table instead of a room full of dusty antiques.

They were supposed to be taking it ease today. Barry planned on disappearing into the background for once, blending, observing, maybe even relaxing. But no. Eric decided they needed to "clear their minds" by bidding on dead people's stuff. Something about "reconnecting with history" and "getting inspired."

Barry leaned back slightly, arms crossed, scanning the room. Overdressed socialites pretending they understood provenance. Collectors murmuring over appraised values. And a man in the corner who looked entirely too interested in the porcelain dogs on Lot 117.

He exhaled slowly. Just another day protecting a billionaire with too much money, too much curiosity, and zero concept of what 'low profile' meant.

"I don't care what it is," Eric whispered, already perking up. "If it's from the 1800s and made of paper, brass, or leather. I want it."

"Why?" Barry muttered.

"Because craftsmanship," Eric replied reverently. "Beauty. Legacy."

Barry rolled his eyes. "You like shiny things you can stack on shelves like trophies."

Eric shrugged. "You're not wrong."

The auctioneer's voice filled the room like a foghorn wrapped in tweed.

"Lot 126! A rare original volume of *Souvenirs of Travel* by Madame Octavia Walton LeVert, Southern author and socialite. Early edition. Beautifully bound. Gilded spine. Original marbling. A seminal work in early female American literature."

Eric's paddle was halfway up before the auctioneer even finished the description.

"Three hundred," someone called.

"Four," Eric said, hardly glancing up.

"Five-fifty," a woman's voice snapped with crisp precision.

Barry turned, mid-eye-roll.

And froze.

There she stood.

Fierce. Bookish. Clearly annoyed. Long curly hair framed her face in wild waves, like intellect on the edge of rebellion. Sharp brown eyes glinted behind tortoiseshell glasses, the kind with a vintage flair that said she knew exactly who she was. She wore a smart navy dress and practical heels—dressed like she might teach a lecture before dismantling your argument over espresso.

She looked like someone who alphabetized her vinyl and wasn't afraid to stab you with a bookmark.

Eric's eyebrows lifted slightly. His lips quirked into a grin, the kind he reserved for rare art, unexpected charm, or an especially attractive pastry.

"Seven hundred," he said, raising his paddle again.

"Eight," the woman replied without missing a beat, her voice as steady as a metronome set to "not here to play."

Barry leaned toward him. "You're bidding against someone who knows what the book means. Not what it matches."

Eric whispered back, "It's going to look amazing between Marcus Aurelius and *Ulysses*."

Barry deadpanned, "Because LeVert clearly wanted her life's work shelved between 'confused Greek guy' and 'impossible-to-finish Irish riddle.'"

"Eight-fifty," Eric said aloud, brushing imaginary lint from his lapel with casual flair.

"Nine hundred," she countered. No hesitation. No smile.

Barry muttered under his breath,

"Two scholars in a field of fools,

One bids for heart, one bids for jewels."

Barry watched as Eric tilted his head.

"One thousand," he said smoothly.

Silence.

The woman's jaw flexed. Her fingers curled ever so slightly around her paddle, then

slowly lowered it to her lap.

"Sold!" the auctioneer called. "To Mr. Whiff, for one thousand dollars."

Eric leaned back in his chair, arms smugly folded, savoring his small triumph.

Barry shook his head. "You just robbed someone in public."

"Is there a law against that?"

"There should be," Barry said.

They'd nearly made it to the lobby when the sound of sharp heels cut through the chatter followed by a sharper voice.

"Excuse me."

They turned.

She was there, arms crossed, fire smoldering behind her glasses. Her jaw set with the determination of someone who did not let things go.

"You outbid me on a book you don't understand."

Eric blinked, caught somewhere between amusement and curiosity. "You mean *Souvenirs of Travel?*"

"Yes," she snapped. "It's one of the earliest travel memoirs written by a Southern woman. A rare and important work. That copy should be in a library. Not part of someone's aesthetic."

Eric held up his hands in mock surrender. "Hey—I like books. I read some. I buy most. This one's going on my shelf."

She gave him a flat, unimpressed stare. "Tragic."

Eric chuckled, unoffended. In fact, the more she scolded, the more intrigued he became.

She hadn't introduced herself. She wasn't flirting. And yet here she was— bold, brilliant, and absolutely certain he didn't deserve that book.

He stuck out a hand. "Eric."

She inhaled sharply, clearly restraining a lecture.

"I'm Claire. Claire Eidean. Perry Library."

Barry blinked. *Wait a second.* That name rang a bell.

But before he could place it, Eric nodded, polite but clueless. "Eric Whiff."

Claire's brow ticked. "That explains everything."

Barry watched her closely. That name, Eidean. He'd heard it. Maybe in his research, maybe on one of those database hits. His instincts prickled, but nothing clicked.

Claire pointed to the book. "Enjoy your antique ego boost."

And with that, she turned and walked away, curls bouncing like punctuation marks.

Eric watched her go, bemused.

Barry raised an eyebrow. "Still glad you bought the book?"

Eric glanced down at the volume, then back at the retreating figure. "Oh yeah," he murmured. "Best ten-hundred-dollar conversation starter I've ever bought."

Eric looked after her. "She's intense. Cute too."

Barry replied, "She's right."

Eric arched a brow. "You're taking her side?"

Barry didn't answer. He was too busy filing the name Claire Eidean in his mental database.

One more thing for Aidan to investigate.

* * *

Back at the penthouse, Barry perched in the leather armchair like a crow in a minimalist aviary, laptop balanced across his thighs, typing one name:

Claire Eidean.

It started as a reflex. A name that pinged something deep in the archives of his memory the second she'd said it. He couldn't place it right away at the auction house, too many distractions, like Eric whispering about marbled endpapers like they were lingerie.

Now, with the quiet hum of the city outside, Barry dug.

Step 1: The Name.

A few keystrokes and some clever database scraping brought up Claire's professional listing:

Claire Beatrice Eidean, MLIS.

Librarian. Perry Library. Houston, Texas. Specializes in archival systems, administration, 19th-century women's literature.

Barry raised an eyebrow. That tracked. But it wasn't the job that caught his attention; it was the face.

A university staff page had a photo.

Barry leaned forward.

It wasn't *exactly* the same angle, but he knew that face. He had *met* that face.

The coffee shop. The sharp voice. The curly hair.

"I asked for an iced brown sugar oat milk shaken espresso with salted caramel cold foam…"

He could still hear it. Still taste the syrupy concoction she'd left behind.

Barry opened the small notebook he kept in his pocket where he logged odd details, call it paranoia, or practice. He scrolled back a few weeks.

Entry: Coffee Shop, Woman. Corrected barista. Order: iced brown sugar oat milk / salted caramel cold foam. Gave me her wrong drink.

I drank it. Regret.

He stared at it.

Claire Eidean was coffee foam woman.

He huffed through his nose. "Of course she was."

Step 2: The Profile.

Just for curiosity's sake, purely professional curiosity, of course, Barry logged into the shadow-side of TruePair's admin portal, a little backdoor access, courtesy of a favor owed by a guy in data security. Barry hadn't used it much. But tonight? It was justified.

He scrolled through Eric's match history.

Emma Green.

The name was clearly fake. The photo, moody umbrella, partial profile, wasn't much help.

Barry pulled it up beside the Perry Library staff photo.

Tilted the screen slightly. Cross-referenced angles. Cheekbone. Jawline. Nose bridge.

Different lighting. Different vibe.

Same woman.

Barry leaned back and rubbed his jaw.

"Damn."

So, Claire, "librarian with the lecture", was *also* "Emma Green with the salted caramel foam."

And neither Eric nor Claire had the faintest idea.

Step 3: The Decision.

Barry could've texted Eric. Could've dropped the bomb. *She's the match. She's the librarian you just ticked off. She's also the woman whose drink made me reevaluate my stance on oat milk.*

But he didn't.

He shut the laptop and stared at the skyline view from his room.

The truth, he'd learned, was like caffeine: best served slowly.

Because this wasn't just about timing. It was about *them*. And if Eric found out too soon, he'd mess it up, trip over himself trying to apologize for winning a book. Or worse, go fully charming fool and ruin it.

And Claire?

She was the type who didn't handle being blindsided well.

So, Barry did what he always did.

He waited and watched.

And, because he couldn't help himself, he muttered:

"O, what tangled web we weave, when first we text to flirt and deceive."

Then he stood, stretched, and made another note in his small book:

Friday. Moody Grounds. Coffee date.

Watch. Listen. Do not interfere.

(Unless oat milk becomes a threat again.)

* * *

Barry sipped his third cup of plain black coffee like it might save him from the slow-motion train wreck happening two feet away.

Eric Whiff was hunched over his phone, thumbs flying, face lit by the soft glow of the TruePair app.

They had a few hours left before the free trial vanished like Cinderella's coach, and Eric, despite every red flag, was still acting like this was the beginning of something great.

Barry, on the other hand, knew better.

He *knew* the woman on the other end of that chat wasn't some fantasy match created by an algorithm.

She was Claire Eidean. Librarian. Auction warrior. Woman scorned by shelving injustice.

And Eric had no idea.

"Okay," Eric said, glancing up with a boyish grin. "Tell me if this sounds good."

Barry raised an eyebrow.

Eric read: *"So, even though your day was rough, maybe Friday can still be something to look forward to? I'll buy the coffee. You bring that umbrella."*

Barry blinked. "You're referencing a photo she hasn't confirmed is even her face."

Eric looked sheepish. "But what if it is?"

Barry took a slow sip of coffee. "And what if it's the woman who called you a 'decorative capitalist bookshelf hog' three hours ago?"

Eric frowned. "What?"

"Nothing," Barry muttered. "Just… poetic dread."

Eric went back to the chat. On screen, a new message from *Emma* had popped up.

Emma: Sorry I'm being weird. Just family stuff. It's fine.

Eric tapped his thumbs, hesitated, then typed:

Ethan: You don't have to explain. But I'm here if you want to.

Barry read the line over Eric's shoulder and grimaced. "You're trying to be supportive, but you sound like a therapist with a clipboard and a latte."

"I'm being emotionally available!" Eric protested.

Barry gave him a look. "You're being available *adjacent.* And she clearly doesn't want to talk."

Eric sighed. "What am I supposed to say?"

"Sometimes," Barry said dryly, "the best thing to say is nothing. Just don't make it worse."

Emma: I don't know why I told you that. You just seem… safe.

Eric's mouth curved into a small smile.

Barry's stomach sank.

Because he knew *exactly* how safe Claire would feel when she walked into Moody Grounds and discovered her "safe" stranger was Eric Whiff, the antique hoarder who outbid her on a cultural landmark.

Ethan: I'm glad you feel that way. I've really liked talking to you.

Emma's typing bubbles appeared. Disappeared. Appeared again.

Emma: Me too. Honestly, I'm nervous about Friday. What if this ruins it?

Eric tilted his head. "She's nervous. That's good, right?"

Barry didn't answer right away. He was too busy picturing the moment Claire stepped through that café door, iced brown sugar oat milk in hand, and realized she'd signed up to spend an hour with the man who treated *Souvenirs of Travel* like it was book-shaped wallpaper.

Ethan: It won't ruin it. I promise. Just… let it be what it is.

Emma: *You still want keep the mystery going? Not reveal our real selves till the coffee shop?*

Ethan: *Sure. My friend tells me I'm paranoid. Let's go for the surprise. You only live once, right?*

Barry cringed as he watched the screen go still.

No typing bubble.

No response.

Eric finally looked up. "Is it weird that I want this to go well?"

Barry exhaled slowly. "No. It's human."

Eric nodded, quietly hopeful.

Barry stood, mug in hand, and stared out the window toward the twinkling lights of Houston. Somewhere out there, Claire was also staring at a screen, torn between nerves and fury and a library-shaped chip on her shoulder.

This was going to go sideways.

And Barry was going to be the one holding the pieces.

He muttered softly, under his breath:

"Two hearts set sail beneath veils and lies,

Unknowing they meet where misfortune flies."

He took a long sip of coffee and sighed.

Friday was going to be a hell of a day.

Chapter 8

Claire

Claire Eidean was thirty-two minutes early.

Not because she was eager, *definitely not,* but because her nerves woke her before dawn and the walls of her apartment started to close in.

Moody Grounds, the coffee shop near the university, contained its usual mix of stressed students and over-caffeinated professors. Jazz played softly from the speakers. The barista with the nose ring didn't look up when Claire ordered.

"Iced brown sugar oat milk shaken espresso. Salted caramel foam." Claire felt her nerves ease a little as she sipped the familiar brew.

She carried the cup to a corner table near the window, where she saw most of the room in a glance. Ethan – or whoever he was – could easily see her.

Today was the day.

The day she'd meet Ethan Wells – the man behind the fake name - the witty, mysterious stranger who responded to her texts in a caring way, if only briefly. She became more than the responsible middle sister and more than the librarian with too many degrees.

Except now, the app had locked her out.

The free trial was over. TruePair was done searching for a match unless she committed with her credit card.

There'd be no confirmation texted, no "just parked," no "wearing a blue sweater." They didn't exchange numbers yet. She wondered if the dark green car that passed by belonged to him.

Just a time.

Just a place.

And two blurry photos between them. While neither of them ever admitted their names were fake on TruePair, she thought it was now understood.

Claire sipped her coffee and tried to keep calm. She wouldn't panic if he didn't show. Wouldn't freak out if he looked nothing like his photo. Wouldn't stay longer than fifteen minutes if he turned out to be another charming narcissist with a strong jaw and weak convictions.

The door chimed.

She glanced up.

And froze.

There, stepping into the sunlit doorway like a glitch in the universe, was Eric Whiff, the man from the auction. The man who outbid her on *Souvenirs of Travel*.

Tall. T-Shirt with a nice blazer. Designer boots. Brows slightly furrowed in confusion.

Claire instinctively leaned back into the shadows of the coffee shop wall, her hand tightening around her drink.

What was *he* doing here?

Mr. Antique Shelf himself.

He scanned the room.

Looking for someone. Looking in her direction.

Looking like *he* was waiting for someone.

No.

No. No. No.

He couldn't be,

Eric pulled out his phone, tapped it, frowned. He turned to another man who followed behind. He was with him the other day, as well. Yet she knew him from someplace else.

Claire's heart kicked.

He was looking for someone indeed.

Was *he* here for her?

She gripped the table. Her coffee shook in its cup.

No. That was impossible. Ethan, her *Ethan*, was warm, open, honest. A little awkward, but sincere. This was Eric Whiff, the man who had outbid her, condescended to her. Moreover, he had walked off with a first edition as if it were decorative wallpaper. The billionaire playboy who appeared in online newsfeeds.

He started walking toward her.

Their eyes met.

He smiled, hesitant, unsure.

She didn't return it. Her breath caught.

And then,

"Emma?" came from Eric.

"Claire?" The voice behind her made her spine straighten.

It wasn't Eric's.

It was Chloe.

Claire turned, heart skipping in a completely different rhythm.

Her youngest sister stood just behind her, backpack slung over one shoulder, hoodie half-zipped, a wary expression behind eyes that looked just like their mother's before the MS had dimmed them.

"Chloe?" Claire breathed. "What, what are you doing here?"

"I needed to talk to you," Chloe said, voice low. "Now."

Claire opened her mouth, stunned.

And then Eric was in front of her, appearing dazed and confused.

"Hi, sorry, are you Emma?" he asked, glancing between the two women. "Claire? Is that what she said? Is that your name? From the auction?"

Claire looked at him. Then at Chloe. Then back.

"This is *not* happening," she muttered under her breath.

The man with Eric moved closer, seeing a change in the situation.

Eyes sharp as if watching for danger.

This wasn't just a date anymore.

This was a storm front.

* * *

Claire blinked between them. Eric was standing with a hesitant smile and soft eyes that didn't match the man she'd met at the auction, and Chloe, arms crossed and already squinting like she'd walked into the wrong episode of someone else's drama.

"What is happening?" Claire breathed, the words more fog than voice.

Chloe stepped closer, giving Eric a quick once-over. "Claire? Who is this guy?"

Eric opened his mouth, then closed it again, clearly sensing this was a bad time, possibly one of the worst. "So, you are Claire Eidean?"

She stood, torn between too many collisions: past, present, reality, and illusion.

Eric offered a small, self-deprecating shrug. "Hi. I think we were supposed to meet?" He paused. "From the app."

Claire couldn't speak. Her brain hadn't caught up.

The man who quoted poetry with her over text. Who said the right thing when she opened up about Mom. The man who hadn't felt like a stranger at all.

He was standing in front of her.

She stared at him like he'd morphed into two different people. In a way, he had.

"I didn't know," she finally whispered. "That it was you."

"I didn't either," he said, gently. "But then I saw you, and…"

He let out a breath and gave a soft, almost sad laugh. "I think I screwed this up before it started."

Chloe looked between them. "Wait. You two were…what?"

Neither answered.

Eric reached into his pocket, pulled out a pen, of course it was sleek, probably made of titanium, and scribbled something on a napkin from her table.

He laid it gently beside Claire's coffee.

"Look, I know we didn't have the best start, Claire. If you ever want to talk again," he said, nodding to the napkin. "That's me. No aliases."

He took a step back. His smile was still kind, but dimmer now. "It was nice meeting you. Even the second time."

Then he turned and walked toward the door.

Claire didn't stop him.

Her fingers hovered over the napkin. His handwriting was annoyingly neat.

He simply wrote, *Eric Whiff,* followed by his personal number.

"Who *was* that? He looks familiar." Chloe asked again, more pointed now.

Claire didn't answer.

Because she didn't know anymore.

Just as the door opened, Claire spotted the man shadowing Eric.

He walked with him, tossed something into the trash, and followed him out.

She watched them both disappear through the glass.

Chloe dropped into the chair across from her, clearly expecting an explanation.

Claire didn't offer one.

Not yet.

She just stared at the napkin and whispered to herself,

"What are the odds?"

* * *

Claire stared at the napkin like it was a riddle.

Eric's number, written in careful, deliberate strokes, sat beside her coffee cup like a secret she hadn't asked for.

Across from her, Chloe was fidgeting, wrapping and unwrapping the drawstring of her hoodie around her finger, her knee bouncing beneath the table like it was running on a separate motor.

"So," Chloe's tone light but eyes sharp, "that guy with the cheekbones and the uncomfortable energy, *should* I ask who he was, or just let you process?"

Claire exhaled, more weary than annoyed. "He's… someone I met online. We were supposed to meet today. I didn't recognize him at first."

Chloe tilted her head. "Well, you looked like someone who spotted their dentist in a horror movie."

Claire gave a faint, humorless smile. "It's complicated."

Chloe let it go. "Everything's complicated with you."

Claire sighed, sometimes Chloe was as bad as Camilia when it came to the judgmental comments.

Silence stretched between them.

Claire broke it. "Why are you here, Chloe?"

The question landed like a quiet explosion. Chloe looked toward the window. A long breath. Then:

"I didn't know where else to go."

Claire waited.

Nothing.

"You disappeared. No calls. A few texts. No explanation. Do you have any idea what that did to Mom?"

"I do," Chloe said softly.

"Then why?"

Chloe's hand reached up and rubbed her jaw, then fell back to the table. "Because I wasn't okay. And I didn't want you to see me so unwell."

Claire's stomach dropped.

"What happened?"

"I fell apart when John left me," Chloe whispered. "I drank too much. Took things that weren't prescribed. Started lying about things I didn't even need to lie about. It got worse, and I pretended it was fine. Until I couldn't pretend anymore."

Claire felt her body go still.

"I checked myself into a residential program last year," Chloe added. "Houston Recovery Center. I was discharged two months ago. I haven't had a drink or anything else since October."

Claire could barely breathe. "Why didn't you call?"

"Because I didn't think I deserved to," Chloe said. "Because I thought you'd already written me off. Camila sure had. And Mom… I couldn't."

Claire stared down at the table, blinking hard.

Chloe pulled a folded paper from her hoodie pocket and slid it across. Claire unfolded it—discharge papers. Proof. Six months clean.

"I'm not asking for anything," Chloe said. "I just needed to tell you the truth. I didn't want you to keep wondering."

Claire looked at her sister, pale, tired, but clearer than she'd ever seen her.

"I don't hate you," she said. "But I'm still angry."

"I can live with that," Chloe said. "I just couldn't live with you not knowing."

Claire swallowed. The foam on her coffee had melted. The number still sat beside the cup.

"I picked today to meet someone new," she said, almost to herself.

"Bad timing?"

Claire snorted. "He's not what I expected. And apparently, I'm not either."

Chloe raised an eyebrow but said nothing.

"Come home with me," Claire said suddenly. "Just for today."

Chloe's posture stiffened as she glanced out the window. "I don't know if I can."

"You don't have to explain anything," Claire said. "Just be there."

After a beat, Chloe nodded.

"Okay."

They stood together. Claire tucked the napkin into her notebook. She didn't know if she'd use the number. Not yet.

But she took it anyway.

* * *

Claire unlocked the door to her apartment, the soft click of the deadbolt echoing in the narrow hallway. She turned to see Chloe still hovering by the stairwell, glancing behind her shoulder like a shadow might detach from the wall and follow them up.

"Chloe?" Claire said gently.

She flinched slightly at her name, then offered a thin smile and hurried inside, brushing past Claire with a bundle of tension in her shoulders. Her small backpack, grubby, worn, and zipped to bursting, bounced against her back as she moved straight to the windows.

Claire closed the door quietly and leaned against it, watching as her younger sister checked each window lock with practiced movements. Then she dropped to her knees and peeked through the blinds like she expected someone to be watching from across the street.

"You want to tell me what's going on?" Claire asked, keeping her voice low.

"I need to lay low for a while," Chloe said, her eyes still trained outside.

"Chloe, this isn't just you 'laying low.' You're twitching like a rabbit in a thunderstorm. Are you in trouble?"

Chloe turned, her gaze sharp. "Not the kind you're thinking. I'm clean, Claire. For real this time."

Claire folded her arms. "Then why are you acting like someone's following you?"

Chloe hesitated. Her eyes darted to the backpack she'd dropped near the couch.

Claire followed her gaze, and her voice softened. "Is someone after you?"

Chloe opened her mouth, then closed it again. "It's not just about me," she whispered.

Claire took a step forward. "What does that mean?"

But Chloe shook her head and walked past her, heading into the kitchen. She opened a cabinet and pulled out a glass, filling it shakily from the tap. Claire followed, not pushing, yet. The silence between them stretched, taut and fragile. She glanced around for Oliver, but he was not in the room with them, hiding somewhere.

Finally, Chloe spoke. "I was helping…someone. Someone who didn't want help, but didn't deserve what happened to them. But I thought if I could find them, get them somewhere safe, maybe I could… fix something. For once."

Claire frowned. "You mean like a friend?"

Chloe gave a small, humorless laugh. "Something like that."

She waited, but Chloe didn't elaborate. Instead, she took a long drink of water and stared out the window again.

Claire exhaled. "Chloe, whatever you're running from… you're not alone here, okay?"

Chloe nodded slowly, but the tremble in her fingers gave her away. She was afraid. More afraid than Claire had ever seen her.

Claire had a terrible feeling whatever she had gotten herself into, it was far from over. This was confirmed when she got up the next morning to find the couch, where Chloe slept, empty and blankets folded nicely on the end.

Claire prayed she'd remember her family still cared.

Chapter 9

Barry

Barry Poet didn't believe in soulmates. Not because he was cynical, though he was, but because people lied. They curated versions of themselves, projected shiny avatars into the world, and expected connection from illusion.

But even he admitted, when Eric Whiff froze at the entrance of Moody Grounds, something real shifted in the air.

Barry clocked her the moment they walked in. Claire Eidean, poised at a corner table, curly hair balanced on the top of her head as if a crown, her drink in hand. He saw her first. But it was Eric who reacted like he'd taken a punch to the solar plexus.

"She's here," Eric murmured.

Barry didn't need to ask who. Claire/Emma sat by the window with the sunlight catching in her hair and the cold foam of her signature drink clinging to the lip of the cup. Of course, it was her. Barry knew since the auction.

Eric, for once, looked completely unsure.

"I can't go up to her," he said under his breath.

Barry tilted his head. "Didn't stop you from outbidding her on a first edition and then ghosting her on TruePair."

"That was different. That was before."

Barry kept his tone neutral. "Still is. She doesn't know it's you."

Eric hesitated, then took a step forward. Claire looked up.

The way her expression changed, from neutral to instant dread, told Barry everything.

Then the stranger walked up. The awkward exchange. Things were not going well.

Now they were back in the SUV, Eric in the passenger seat, staring straight ahead like he'd forgotten how to blink.

Barry merged into traffic, letting the silence stretch. He could taste the tension in the air, hot, awkward, dense with the kind of regret that didn't go away with a drink.

"That was her," Eric finally said.

"I gathered."

Eric exhaled, the kind of sound a man makes when he's trying to reassemble his dignity from the sidewalk.

"She hates me."

Barry changed lanes. "She didn't throw her coffee at you."

Eric gave a weak laugh. "That's your bar now?"

"With you? Absolutely."

Eric groaned, dragging his hand down his face. "Ugg, I made such an idiot of myself at that auction."

"You did," Barry agreed.

"She knew the book. She loved the book. And I shelved it like it was some… ornament."

Barry gave a soft grunt. "A true crime."

Eric slouched lower. "And now she thinks I'm a liar."

"You are," Barry said evenly. "But so is she."

Eric shot him a look.

"Fake names, remember?" Barry reminded him. "She didn't tell you who she was either. You both showed up wearing masks. Though that other person walking up caught me off guard. Did she say who she was?"

"No," said Eric and then he fell silent.

Barry glanced over at a red light. "You want my advice?"

"Not really, but you're going to give it anyway."

"Let her be mad," Barry said. "Let her process. You gave her your number. That was the right move."

Eric nodded slowly. "You think she'll call?"

"Nope."

Eric's expression sank.

"But," Barry added, "she might still read the napkin."

Eric looked at him.

"You don't fix this with charm," Barry said. "You fix it with truth. And patience. And not acting like the guy who buys first editions for show."

Eric turned back to the window, jaw tight. "I want to fix it."

"Then stop being surprised that something real requires work."

The light turned green.

Barry drove on, the road stretching ahead of them like a quiet challenge. And then, almost to himself, he said:

"The truth will out where silence fails,

But only if the heart prevails."

Eric sighed. "Do you write these down somewhere?"

Barry smirked. "Nah. Just collect 'em like bruises."

They didn't speak the rest of the ride back.

But Barry knew it wasn't over.

* * *

Barry didn't mind running interference. It was, after all, the bulk of his job. But delivering an apology gift to a woman who'd just discovered her TruePair mystery man was also her book-collecting nemesis and wealthy? That required finesse and a lot of caffeine.

Eric hadn't got out of the car after they parked. He sulked for days after the coffee shop meeting, much to Barry's annoyance, and now they were outside the Perry Library. Instead of focusing on his work, Barry watched Eric scroll through the old texts with Emma/Claire during their high-speed rail meetings.

Barry leaned against the driver's side door and crossed his arms. "So, you want me to do what, exactly?"

"Tell her the truth, that I want to donate the book. No strings, no press. Let her know I get it now." Eric hesitated, then added, "And that I hope it's not too late."

Barry nodded slowly. "You want redemption, and you're outsourcing it."

Eric gave him a look. "You're better with words."

Barry grunted. "Only when I'm not using someone else's."

With a sigh, Barry closed the car door and turned toward the Perry Library.

Inside, it was cooler than expected. The marble floors dominated the silence and the comforting scent of old pages. Students moved like shadows between the shelves. Upstairs, past the circulation desk and down a narrow corridor, he found the right office. Frosted nameplate: Claire Eidean, Administration, Special Collections.

He knocked once.

Claire opened the door a few inches, clearly not expecting company. Her eyes narrowed the moment she saw him.

"You," she said.

Barry gave a small nod. "Me."

She opened the door fully, arms folded. "What now?"

"I come in peace," Barry said, holding up both hands. "Eric's not with me."

"Good," she muttered.

Barry added. "My name is Barry Poet. He didn't want to corner you. Didn't want to seem like he was following you. He's rather well known, you know."

Claire arched a brow. "Sending his friend isn't exactly less weird."

Barry gave her a dry smile. "Fair. It probably doesn't make it better, but I'm his bodyguard. I am not coming with flowers or apologies. Just a gift."

He reached into the large pocket inside his jacket and pulled out a wrapped bundle, laying it gently on the edge of her desk.

"He's donating the book he won in the auction," Barry said. "*Souvenirs of Travel.* Full transfer. No fanfare, no plaques, no speeches. Just… where it belongs."

Claire blinked, her expression unreadable.

"He wanted you to know it wasn't about winning," Barry continued. "And that he's sorry for how it all looked, at the auction, and after. He may be an idiot, but he's not the same kind of idiot he used to be."

Claire opened the bundle, skimming the rare book in her hands. Barry watched as her eyes moved over the volume, its small details, authenticity, crisp pages, gilded edges.

"This is real," she said softly.

"It is."

Claire set the book down, her fingers lingering on the edge of the desk. "Why are you doing this?"

Barry hesitated. Then he said, "Because he listened. And maybe because I've come to believe in unlikely things. Like men who read poetry and women who remember coffee orders better than names."

Claire almost smiled. Almost.

Barry stepped back. "He left his number. You already have it. But he said he'd understand if you never used it."

Claire didn't respond. Not immediately.

Barry gave a slight bow, half-joking, half-respectful, and added, in his usual quiet cadence:

"He who shelves the book alone

Learns too late what could be known."

Then he left her standing there, sunlight filtering through the high library windows, the book in her hands.

Barry left the building, walked through the parking lot, and opened the drivers side door.

Eric looked over as Barry climbed back into the SUV, shutting the door with a soft *click*.

"Well?" Eric asked, voice low.

Barry set his sunglasses on the dash. "She took it."

Eric queried, "Did she, did she ask why?"

"She didn't have to." Barry glanced over at him. "I told her it was from you, free and clear. That you wanted her to have it. That you knew she cared about it. And that you wanted to do one thing right."

Eric nodded slowly, the weight in his chest not gone, but shifting. "And?"

"She said thank you," Barry said. "She opened the book. Looked at the title page like it was an old friend."

* * *

Barry's phone buzzed again. Not his personal one, his second, encrypted line. The one only his team used to reach him.

Aidan Brooks flashed across the screen.

The kid didn't waste words.

Aidan: *"Encrypted flag hit. C. Eidean. Tied to El Paso network. Targeted. Direct language used."*

Barry stilled.

Everything shifted.

Eric was in the passenger seat, foot tapping out a nervous, uneven rhythm against the floor mat. Barry was about to tell him they should pull back, give Claire breathing room, but the text changed everything.

He hit call.

"Aidan. Talk."

The voice on the other end was calm, clipped, a younger version of Barry's own restraint. "Keyword was 'Eidean.' Packet intercept. Chatroom scrub flagged her name, tied to known El Paso thread. It's not abstract. It's a mark."

Barry's spine straightened. "How certain?"

"Eighty-seven percent confidence. Language is too specific for coincidence. No mistaking the target. They're moving."

Barry didn't hesitate. "Location?"

"Public building. Perry Library."

"On it."

He ended the call and stepped out into the bright Texas heat, moving fast.

Eric was already turning. "What?"

Barry leaned back just enough to meet his gaze. "Claire. There's a threat.

Direct, credible, linked to encrypted chatter out of El Paso. Her name was used. They're planning something."

Eric was out of the SUV before Barry finished the sentence.

"Then what the hell are we doing here?"

Barry didn't reply. He was already crossing the plaza.

The library loomed ahead, sunlight bouncing off the glass like a warning. Inside, everything looked still, too still. The kind of calm that precedes chaos.

Barry stepped in first, eyes scanning. Fluorescent lights buzzed. A printer clacked. And there, just outside Claire's office, a man leaned against the wall.

Arms crossed.

Too casual.

Barry's instincts kicked in.

In one swift move, he closed the distance, locked an arm around the man's neck, and pinned him to the wall with controlled force.

"Say a name," Barry growled. "Say why you're here."

The man gasped. "Zak, I'm Zak, Circulation Department, I swear, printer maintenance!"

Barry didn't let go.

Then,

"Hey, you big nut!" Claire's voice, sharp with alarm.

She rushed forward, eyes wide. "What are you doing to Zak?! What are you doing back here?!"

Zak coughed. "I was only fixing her paper tray! Honest!"

Barry released him.

Claire stepped in, shielding Zak with a glare. "He's harmless."

Barry stayed calm. "We got word. You were named in a credible threat. We're not taking chances."

Claire blinked. "Me? Why me?"

Eric stepped beside her, voice steady. "We don't know. But it's real. Barry is the best, and we need to move. Now."

Claire's gaze darted between them. Then she nodded once. "Give me thirty seconds." Zak had since disappeared, probably rushing to alarm campus police.

She grabbed her bag.

The intercom crackled overhead.

"Ms. Claire Eidean, you have a visitor in the main lobby."

Barry's eyes sharpened. "Don't go. Move. Now."

They pushed through a staff stairwell, down toward the basement exit. Every step felt loud. Exposed.

Outside, the sun still burned, but something colder had taken root.

They reached the SUV. Claire slid into the passenger seat, jaw tight. Eric followed to the back seat.

Barry landed in the driver's seat and drove off campus.

No one spoke for the first three blocks.

Then Barry broke the silence.

"I'll contact Aidan. He's already flagging external traffic logs, burner chatter, anything that leads us closer. We'll know who made the call."

Claire finally turned toward him. "Who's Aidan?"

"My...friend," Barry said. "Bright. Scary smart. Learns fast. He's the reason we're here now."

Claire nodded slowly.

Barry didn't take his eyes off the road. "You've been pulled into something that predates this morning. El Paso's just the surface. This goes deeper."

"Deeper how?"

Barry exhaled. "We don't know why you are on their radar or who clearly 'they' are."

Claire paled.

Barry drove on, fast, clean, precise.

And as the skyline fell behind them, he muttered under his breath:

"First the name, then the shadow's shape.

But this time, they won't escape."

Because now it was personal.

And no one hurt the people under Barry Poet's protection.

Not while he still had breath.

Chapter 10

Claire

"Okay," Claire snapped, spinning in her seat to face Barry. "You need to tell me what's going on. Now."

Barry kept his eyes locked on the road. "You've been flagged. Your name came up in an intercepted threat."

Claire blinked. "Flagged? By who? The Library of Congress?" Her tone was biting, incredulous.

Eric, from the back seat, leaned forward slightly, voice low. "He's not joking, Claire."

"Private channel," Barry said, jaw tight. "Fixer out of El Paso. Former military intel. Clean source. The message was direct."

Claire twisted to look between the two of them. "My name?"

Barry gave a single nod. "C. Eidean."

Claire let out a sharp, disbelieving laugh. "That doesn't even make sense."

"What part doesn't?" Barry asked.

"There are three C. Eideans," she said, counting on her fingers. "I'm the middle one. Camila's older, Chloe's younger. That initial could mean any of us. Did your contact say *Claire*? Or are we doing this over a single letter and a vibe you picked up over breakfast?"

Eric leaned forward, resting his elbows on the center console. "Claire, come on. You really think Barry moves on a hunch?"

She turned on him, frustration flaring. "You're not helping."

"I'm not trying to help," Eric shot back. "I'm trying to keep you alive."

Claire narrowed her eyes. "Based on what? A vague note with a single initial?"

Barry cut in, his voice firm. "It wasn't just the initial. The message said, *'Watch for C. Eidean. She knows more than she should.'*"

Claire went still. Her breath caught mid-argument.

Eric's voice dropped. "That sounds personal."

She looked away, jaw clenched. "They could still mean Camila. Or Chloe."

Before Barry could reply, there was a ring. Barry picked up the phone, Claire catching the words, "Boss, it's Aidan."

Barry pressed the speaker. "Go."

"I ran the chatter through the new decryption layer. Whoever this fixer is, they didn't drop a name. They included a timestamp and a location tag. It pinged your last known coordinates."

Claire's face paled. "Wait. That was my office. You think someone's been tracking *me*?"

"It's possible," Aidan replied. "We also intercepted a second thread. It referenced the name 'Claire' directly, once. Casual phrasing, but too specific to ignore."

Barry's grip tightened on the wheel. "Send it to my secondary line. Pull the old traffic cams on the university lot. And cross-check staff access logs for the last twenty-four hours."

"On it," Aidan said. "And Barry, this one feels different."

Barry's jaw flexed. "I know."

The call cut off.

Claire stared out the window for a beat, trying to keep her voice level. "So now what?"

Barry didn't hesitate. "Now, we get off the grid. Lock it down. You, your mother, Camila and anyone else - we all go dark. Until I know which Eidean they're after, I'm assuming they're after all three."

Claire swallowed. "What about Camilia's kids, husband, and Chloe?"

Barry glanced at her, eyes unreadable. "Everyone. Chloe might've known this was coming, you know."

Claire's hand tightened around the seatbelt strap. "And if she left a trail…?"

Barry gave a grim nod. "Then we follow it. Carefully. But first, I keep you alive."

Claire narrowed her eyes. "Why did they specify *me*?"

"No idea. But the context pointed to you, your workplace, your schedule."

She let out a bitter breath. "So, you tackled the Circulation guy and yanked me out of my job based on a *feeling*?"

"It wasn't a feeling," Barry said, voice hardening. "It was a direct threat and your name. I'm not risking your life to wait for clarity."

Claire turned her face to the window. "You really don't do small talk, do you?"

"Small talk doesn't stop bullets," Barry muttered.

They drove in silence for a few blocks, the road humming beneath the tires. She could feel the tension rolling off Eric in the back seat like static, but she wasn't ready to deal with him yet.

"Chloe's been acting strange for over a year," Claire said. "Paranoid. Kept checking the windows at my apartment the other night. She told me she was helping someone but wouldn't say who. What if she's the one in danger? Or worse, what if she brought it to *me*?"

Then something cracked open in her thoughts.

Her eyes slowly returned to Barry. "You knew my real name before the coffee shop."

His silence confirmed it.

"You *knew* I was Emma," she said, voice sharp.

From the back seat, Eric jerked forward. "Wait, what?"

Claire turned in her seat just as Eric leaned forward between them, his voice stunned. "You *knew*?"

"Yes," Barry said calmly.

Claire and Eric responded at the same time, voices overlapping:

"Since when?!"

"For how long?!"

Barry glanced between them.

They both stared at him.

Claire's voice dropped to a razor's edge. "And you didn't think either of us deserved to *know*?"

"I thought it would come out naturally," Barry replied. "If either of you had a chance, I couldn't force it."

"Oh," Claire said, laughter bubbling up from disbelief. "You're a romantic now. Great."

Eric rubbed a hand across his face. "I can't believe this Barry."

"I'm not the enemy here," Barry said.

Claire turned toward the windshield. "No. You're just the guy who watched this whole mess unfold like a spectator at a slow-motion train crash."

Neither of them spoke for a moment.

Eric let out a breath. "We trusted you."

"I protected you," Barry replied. "Both of you."

Claire stared out the window as the city streamed past, the world outside unchanged while everything inside the car unraveled.

* * *

Barry's phone buzzed sharply against the console.

Claire didn't recognize the tone, but the way his entire body stilled told her all she needed to know, this wasn't casual. He answered the call without a word.

"You still with her?" a clipped voice asked.

"Yes," Barry replied.

Claire leaned a fraction closer, her pulse ticking up.

"Good. Because it's worse than we thought."

Barry's knuckles tightened on the wheel. "How bad?"

"They've got two addresses tagged with the name 'C. Eidean.' One near the university. One in Travis Heights. The chatter's not passive anymore, they're coordinating. Movement could happen tonight."

Claire felt the blood drain from her face.

"Confirmed target?" Barry asked.

"No. However, recent search activity narrows it down to either Claire or the younger one. Chloe."

Barry's jaw worked as he absorbed that. "Aliases on the players?"

"Just handles. But they're professionals. You need to disappear her. Quietly."

Before Barry could respond, a second voice cut in, clear, younger, with the quick cadence of someone used to monitoring a dozen screens at once.

"Barry, it's Aidan," the junior assistant interjected. "I'm backtracking the forum posts linked to the pings. Whoever's behind this knows how to scrub, but they made one slip on an IP relay bounce. I think we've got a partial fingerprint."

Barry's voice remained steady. "Location?"

"Somewhere near El Paso. Industrial subnet. Same one flagged two weeks ago."

Barry nodded. "Good work. Keep eyes on both flagged addresses. Loop facial rec from any outbound feeds and notify me the second anything shifts."

"Already compiling," Aidan replied. "But Barry? This isn't amateur hour. These guys know what they're doing."

"Yeah," Barry said grimly. "So do we."

The call ended with a sharp click. Barry didn't move for a second, then set the phone back in the console and blew out a slow breath.

Claire stared at him. "Let me guess. Change of plans?"

"Correct."

"Of course."

"You're not going back to your apartment."

She turned sharply. "Excuse me?"

"Both your place and Travis Heights are hot. They have your names. Your addresses."

Claire blinked. "Travis Heights is my mother's house. Camila and the kids live there."

Eric shifted in the back seat. "Are they safe?"

Barry didn't look at him. "We don't know yet. I'm taking Claire somewhere secure."

Claire folded her arms. "Where, exactly?"

Barry answered, calm as ever. "Eric's penthouse."

Claire froze. But Eric beat her to the punch.

"I'm sorry, *what* now?" he said, leaning forward like Barry suggested building a bunker in his living room.

"Top floor, private elevator, three layers of security, rooftop surveillance, bulletproof glass," Barry listed, ticking them off like menu items.

Eric threw up a hand. "I've got priceless art and a designer white sofa."

Barry glanced at him in the mirror. "And now you've got guests."

Claire blinked, then let out a short, almost hysterical laugh. "Fantastic. From book auction nemesis to anonymous flirtation to panic room. What's next, matching pajamas and a livestream apology tour?"

Eric muttered, "Let's not give media any ideas."

Barry ignored them both and made a sharp turn. "We'll stop by Claire's apartment. Grab essentials. Move fast."

Claire crossed her arms. "I'm not leaving without my cat."

Barry paused. "Your... cat?"

"I knew it," she heard Eric exclaim from the back seat.

"Oliver. Spotted tux. Four legs, judgmental eyes, lives to knock things off tables."

Eric sighed like he'd just remembered he owned fragile figurines.

"Well, at least he's not a Winston," replied Barry as he suppressed a laugh.

Claire added, "Of course that's not his name. Also requires his special diet and a litter box. And yes, I will be packing both."

Barry was silent for a moment. "Anything else?"

"My laptop, hard drive, a few clothes, books," she said. Then, dryly, "Maybe some dignity."

Eric said under his breath, "You won't find any of that in the laundry pile."

Claire gave him a sidelong glare. "Keep talking and I'll leave Oliver in *your* room."

Barry, still stone-faced, said, "You've got twenty minutes. I sweep. You pack. We leave. Deal?"

"Deal."

Claire paused, then quietly asked, "You're serious about this?"

Barry's tone was steel. "Someone is planning something ugly. And you're in the crosshairs. This isn't a drill."

Claire nodded tightly. But the real fear came rushing back. "What about Camila? My mom?"

Barry didn't answer right away; his eyes were already scanning the road, watching for anything that didn't belong.

"We get your things," he said. "Then we call your sister."

The SUV pulled up outside her apartment complex. Claire's heart pounded. Not because she was scared, though she was, but because this was real. Tangible. Her world was shifting, and the street outside her building felt foreign.

Barry stepped out first, his hand hovering near his hip, already in protective mode.

And just as he rounded the front of the SUV, she heard him mutter under his breath:

"Guard the heart, though the walls may fall,

Even the hunted must rise and stall."

Claire blinked.

Eric, from the back seat, muttered, "If he starts reciting more poetry, I'm going to need a drink."

Claire managed a half-smile as she opened her door.

* * *

Barry entered first, sweeping the apartment building like it was second nature, one hand grazing the walls, the other near his hip, eyes scanning corners, shadows, windows, exits. Claire barely turned the lock to her apartment before he was inside moving room to room, clearing the space like it might vanish under his boots.

Behind him, Claire pushed the door open the rest of the way, calling, "Oliver? Ollie, baby, where are you?"

Her heart already racing, not from fear, but from the sheer chaos of trying to shove her life into twenty minutes of tactical panic.

Eric followed close behind, ducking under the doorframe and scanning the apartment like someone who'd never stepped inside a home that wasn't dressed in curated marble and security glass.

Barry's voice floated from the kitchen. "Living room clear. Kitchen clear. Hallway good."

Claire didn't wait as she dropped her keys into the bowl by the door, kicked off her shoes, and headed straight for the bedroom.

"He always hides when the carrier comes out," she muttered. "Like he *knows.*"

She dropped to her knees and peered under the bed. Nothing. Then,

Two glowing green eyes blinked back at her.

A shape flattened itself farther into the shadows.

Barry crouched beside her a moment later. "He knows," he said dryly. "He's judging us both."

Claire shook the treat bag like a maraca. "Come on, you little drama queen. We don't have time for this."

She tossed a few treats under the bed with zero dignity. The cat didn't budge.

Barry stood and disappeared again, ghosting silently back down the hall.

Eric, still awkwardly standing near the bookcase, turned in a slow circle. "This is… cozy."

Claire glanced up at him. "That's code for 'small,' isn't it?"

"No! No," Eric said too quickly. "It's… lived in. And aggressively alphabetical."

She sighed and stood. "I *like* knowing where things are."

Eric opened a book at random, revealing four Post-its stuck to one paragraph. "I can tell."

Claire left him and moved toward the closet. She flipped it open and pulled her go-to suitcase from the top shelf. As it hit the bed, the zipper slipped open slightly.

And there it was.

A soft, worn canvas tote.

Claire froze. Her chest tightened.

Chloe's bag.

She pulled it out slowly, thumb brushing across the familiar faded strap.

Her sister must've stashed it here. The other night? Before she left?

Had she forgotten it, or left it behind on purpose?

Voices buzzed behind her, but she couldn't hear the words. Only the rising tide of questions.

She looked toward the hallway. Barry was still out of sight. Eric had wandered into the kitchen, poking at her French press like it might bite him.

Without a word, Claire slipped the tote back into the suitcase and tugged a shirt over it. She didn't say anything. Not yet.

Now wasn't the time.

She threw things on top, jeans, a few comfortable shirts, her favorite worn sweater, a book with a cracked spine, and the black t-shirt she always wore when she needed to look tougher than she felt.

Down the hallway, claws clicked against hardwood.

Oliver had emerged, cautiously sniffing the air.

Barry's voice drifted in. "We've got maybe twelve minutes."

Claire dropped everything and lunged. "Now, Oliver!"

The cat bolted, but she was faster.

She caught him mid-air, limbs flailing, a full-body hiss erupting in protest.

"Don't you *dare*," she muttered, wrangling his furry fury into the crate like a seasoned rodeo pro. The second the latch clicked, he howled like he'd been betrayed by the only person he ever trusted.

"You'll live," she said, breathless.

Eric reappeared in the doorway, eyebrows raised. "Remind me not to cross you."

Claire wiped her arm across her forehead. "Honestly, this is tame."

Barry returned from the bedroom with her suitcase in hand, eyes sweeping the space one final time.

"All clear," he said. "Nothing disturbed."

Claire nodded, hefting the crate as Oliver continued his operatic protest. "He's in. Food and litter are packed."

Eric moved to the door and held it open. "I'll carry your emotional support demon if you want."

Claire smirked. "He bites."

Eric smirked right back. "I've survived worse."

Together, they stepped into the hallway, Claire juggling Oliver's food and a grocery bag of cat gear, Barry cool and steady, Eric, Oliver's crate in hand, still visibly trying to process the fact that he was about to let this entire circus into his penthouse.

None of them looked back.

* * *

The SUV sliced through Houston's streets, headlights sweeping across empty sidewalks and shuttered windows. Barry gripped the wheel like he was holding the city itself steady. Claire sat stiffly beside him, phone in her lap, screen dim, her thumb hovering over Camila's name.

The hum of the engine filled the silence.

"Call her," Barry said without looking away from the road.

Claire nodded once and tapped the screen.

It rang. Once. Twice.

Then: "Claire?" Camila's voice cut through the quiet, already frazzled. "What's going on?"

Claire opened her mouth, but Barry extended a hand.

She passed him the phone without question.

"Camila, this is Barry Poet," he said, tone calm but no-nonsense.

A pause. Then a sharp suspicion. "Who?"

"I'm with Claire. We haven't met, but I need you to listen to me."

"Where's Charles?" asked Claire.

"Still in Dallas for that gaming convention, right?" Barry asked, not missing a beat.

Camila hesitated. "Yeah… Why do you know that?"

"Connections. You're alone and we need to keep you and your family safe," Barry said.

Barry's voice dropped, low and steady. "Camila, I need you to pack a bag. You, the kids, and your mom. Be ready in fifteen minutes. We're coming to get you."

There was silence. Then: "I'm sorry, *who the hell are you again?*"

Claire leaned closer. "He's someone I trust. Please, Camila. Don't argue. Just do it. I'll explain everything when we get there."

A longer pause this time.

"Fine," Camila said. "But this better not be one of your weird drama things."

Barry muttered, "It always is," and ended the call.

Claire sat back, exhaling slowly as she placed the phone in the cupholder.

Next to her, Barry's eyes never left the road. In the rearview mirror, she could see Eric watching her, quiet, unsure, but not indifferent.

"You think this is connected to Chloe?" she asked, her voice barely above a whisper.

"I can't think of any other reason," Barry said. "You said she was shaking when she showed up. Looking over her shoulder. That kind of fear comes from experience, not imagination."

Claire felt her stomach twist. "What if she didn't mean to bring this with her?"

Barry commented. "Doesn't matter. The road to hell is paved with good intentions."

The words hit her like cold water.

She turned toward the windshield. The streetlights flickered across Barry's face in gold streaks, shadows catching beneath his cheekbones. He didn't look nervous. He looked ready.

They all fell silent as the neighborhoods grew more familiar. School signs. The corner market. The crooked streetlamp at the end of Camila's block.

Then Barry spoke again, almost like an invocation:

"When silence breaks beneath a name,
The hunters come, but not for fame."

Eric let out a slow breath. "Is that something you made up, or something we should worry about?"

Barry didn't answer.

Claire didn't need him to.

Chapter 11

Eric

The lobby echoed with the sharp, self-assured click of Eric Whiff's polished shoes, each step screaming *executive presence*. Behind him, however, came the unmistakable crazy of real life catching up: the slap-slap of hurried flip-flops, a suitcase thudding rhythmically against every tile, someone barking into a phone about logistics, and what could only be described as a rogue kazoo.

Gregory, the doorman, stood with the poise of a man who had once opened a door for a foreign dignitary and never quite recovered from the pride of it. His uniform was immaculate, his posture military, and his tolerance for nonsense long since smoothed into a blank, professional smile.

But today tested his legendary composure.

His eyebrows arched, slightly, just enough, as he took in the parade trailing behind Eric Whiff. A woman in a wheelchair, pushed forward by a dark-haired lady carrying a large duffle bag. Barry, the bodyguard, held a cat carrier that shook violently and emitted noises suspiciously like a chainsaw. A teenager wrapped in so many charging cords, he looked like a rogue electronics display. Two younger children were mid-battle over what may have once been a single granola bar, now split and equally unsatisfactory to both.

And then came the pièce de resistance: Claire's sister, Camila, dragging a suitcase that could have comfortably housed a canoe, or several bad decisions.

Gregory's eye twitched. Barely. He gave the smallest nod, the kind reserved for heads of state and incoming hurricanes.

"Mr. Whiff," he said smoothly. "You appear to have… acquired company."

Eric gave a tight smile. "Yes. They're with me."

"All of them?" Gregory asked.

Eric leaned in slightly and slid a one-hundred-dollar bill across the podium. "My penthouse. My rules. I trust no one else needs to know about this?"

Gregory blinked, then nodded. "Very good, sir."

The elevator arrived with a chipper *ding*, as if it hadn't just been asked to transport the cast of a traveling circus. As the doors slid shut behind them, chaos settled into a compact, vertical rectangle.

One of the kids immediately lunged for the panel and pressed every single button with glee.

Eric didn't stop him. He just closed his eyes as the elevator chirped like a panicked robot.

He let out a slow, soul-weary breath, the sound of a man gently unraveling. "This is fine," he muttered. "I didn't need peace. Or dignity."

Barry stood beside him, clutching the cat carrier at arm's length like it might explode. It hissed again, loud enough to make the teenager trip over a phone cord and fall against the wall.

"You're holding up," Barry offered, completely deadpan.

"I'm dissociating," Eric replied. "Somewhere in my mind, I'm alone in the Alps, drinking espresso and pretending I've never met any of these people."

The cat howled. The elevator stopped at the second floor for absolutely no reason. Claire's sister sneezed loudly enough to scare one of the children.

Barry nodded. "Sounds nice. Let me know if your mind has room service."

When the elevator doors slid open to reveal the pristine marble floor and curated lighting of his penthouse, Eric stepped out into what used to be his sanctuary.

Claire wheeled her mother toward the windows in quiet grace. "Mom can look out while we get her room ready. Which room has the bathroom closest to the bed?"

Eric watched her go from room to room, he had eight bedrooms in this suite, looking for the perfect one. It was obvious how much she cared, but the family was overwhelmed with Beatrice's care. They needed help and his connection at the local hospital could advise him on what to do.

Barry trailed after Claire, the cat carrier swinging low at his side like a ticking time bomb. Claire opened the door to one of the guest rooms and gently placed Oliver inside to decompress, though judging by the furious yowling, "decompression" was going to be a process.

Camila, meanwhile, was already halfway down the hall, striding like a woman on a house-hunting reality show. She paused briefly at a door, peeked inside, and with an approving nod that screamed *I could make this work*, swept into the room like it already belonged to her.

"Ensuite bathroom," she announced to no one in particular. "I mean, *finally*, some standards."

Barry raised an eyebrow. "Are we assigning rooms or staging a coup?"

Camila ignored him, already fluffing a throw pillow like she was being judged on presentation.

Nathan made a beeline for the living room, eyes locking on the massive flat-screen TV with the speed and precision of a teenager who'd just spotted a console hookup. "Yes!" he shouted, diving for the remote like it owed him money.

Meanwhile, Olivia and Henry took off toward the hallway, mid-argument about who got which guest bedroom. Their voices echoed down the corridor, escalating from "You got the window last time!" to "You snore like a wildebeest!"

Claire sighed and leaned against the doorframe, arms crossed. "This was supposed to be temporary."

Barry smirked, "So was the Roman Empire. Look how that turned out."

Eric stared at the scene unraveling in front of him.

This was no longer an artfully minimalist haven.

It was a living diorama.

"Please tell me someone brought snacks," he muttered as someone in the house yelled they were hungry.

Camila dropped her massive bag on the velvet settee and flopped onto it with a sigh. "The kids have granola bars, and I think I packed chips somewhere. You got drinks?"

Eric opened his mouth, closed it again, and muttered, "I have drinks, but not the kind you give minors. I think I have a case of water somewhere."

Oliver the cat emerged from Claire's room. One of the kids must have let him out, his tail twitching as he began surveying the space like a contractor inspecting shoddy work.

Claire set a large bag of cat food and a sack of canned food in one of the kitchen cabinets. "We'll keep everything contained. I promise."

Barry walked over to inspect the setup. "Containment is relative."

Nathan had already found the remote. "Your TV is bigger than my whiteboard at school."

Eric dragged a hand over his face. "That television is calibrated for film industry color standards."

Nathan shrugged. "Cool."

Claire came to his side, looking tired but grateful. "Thank you again. Really. This means more than you know."

Eric looked around. Claire's mother was settled peacefully by the window. Her sister, Camila, had propped her feet up as though she paid rent. The twins raced down the hall. The cat was eying the imported rug like it might need a trim.

He sighed. "Well. At least the place finally has some sound."

Barry handed him a cup. "Made this from your stash."

Eric took a sip. Whiskey.

He glanced sideways at Barry. "Thanks."

"You look like you needed help."

Claire smiled. "Don't we all?"

Eric studied her a moment. "I think this is the strangest thing I've ever done."

"And yet," Barry said, "you look less miserable than usual."

Claire's smile lingered as she returned to her mother's side.

Eric sank onto the edge of the couch, just missing one of Olivia's sticker books. The couch? Somehow, it didn't feel empty anymore.

He wasn't ready to admit it out loud.

But maybe this, whatever *this* was, might not be the worst kind of disruption.

* * *

The kitchen had never felt warmer.

It wasn't the lighting or the soft hum of appliances. It was Claire. Standing at his counter, one hand wrapped around a steaming mug, the other trailing across the neatly labeled spice rack like she was reading a poem.

"They're in alphabetical order," she murmured.

Eric looked up from rinsing a glass. "Of course they are."

She smiled. "By spice name. Not brand. That's the right way."

He blinked. "You… alphabetize by name?"

"Anything else would be crazy." she said, sipping slowly.

Eric felt an unexpected flicker of admiration, the kind he usually reserved for well-timed train arrivals and balanced investment portfolios.

"I've never met anyone who noticed," he said.

"I notice everything. Bad habit. Or maybe a defense mechanism."

He leaned against the counter across from her, elbows resting on the stone surface. "That must be exhausting."

Claire met his gaze. "It's useful. At least when everything else feels like it's spinning, I can organize books by call number and pretend something's in control."

He understood that more than he cared to admit.

"This place…" she said softly, glancing around. "It's spotless. Immaculate. But not cold. It's organized. That's a hard balance."

He tilted his head. "You sound surprised."

"I figured you'd have a staff keeping everything polished."

"I do," he admitted. "But I reorganize after they leave."

Claire grinned. "Control freak."

"Takes one to know one."

Their laughter met in the middle, quiet, real.

Eric's eyes settled on her, the way she cradled the mug in both hands like it grounded her. In that soft light, her hair loose from the day, she looked entirely out of place in his sleek kitchen, and yet, entirely right.

He stepped just slightly closer.

"You know," he said quietly, "I'm glad you're here."

She looked up, surprised. "Even with the noise and the glitter and the cat plotting vengeance?"

"Even then," he said, voice low.

There was a beat. The kind of moment that teetered between breath and bravery. Claire's smile softened, eyes searching his.

Then,

"CLAIRE!" Camila's voice shattered the quiet.

Footsteps thundered down the hall.

The twins burst into the kitchen like tiny invaders.

"Guess what?" Olivia said, already climbing onto a stool. "We made a house for Oliver out of the pillows from the couch!"

"He didn't like to stay in it and ran to the bathroom in your room!" Henry added.

Claire's eyes widened. "What?!"

Nathan strolled in, chewing on something. "TV's cool. Can I hook up my Switch?"

Camila followed, brushing something off her shirt. "Do you have one of those Tide pens? Claire, I swear Olivia got cheese puff dust on the guest comforter."

Oliver let out a dramatic *mrrrowl* from somewhere down the hall, confirming the report.

Eric watched as the woman who had just been inches from his heart transformed back into the family wrangler she clearly was. Claire handed off her mug, called for Olivia to come down, and moved out of the kitchen in one graceful sweep, like a general returning to the front lines.

She paused in the doorway and looked back at Eric. "We'll finish this later?"

He nodded. "Absolutely. Just don't alphabetize my liquor cabinet."

Her grin lingered as she vanished down the hall.

Eric noticed her forgotten cup of tea on the counter. He decided to try it and took a slow sip.

Still warm.

Still sweet.

* * *

He didn't go back to the living room right away.

Even with the kids finally corralled into rooms and the cat somehow appeased with a new perch near the window, Eric lingered in the kitchen, alone, tracing the rim of Claire's abandoned mug with his thumb.

Crystal crossed his mind. She had gone quiet.

Too quiet.

And in Eric's world, silence was never innocent. It was the breath before a lie, the pause before a punch. He'd seen enough business partners smile while plotting his downfall. Crystal didn't disappear; she calculated. And whatever she planned, it wasn't going to be harmless.

He glanced down at the tablet Barry had left on the counter. The screen had gone black, but Eric could still see the reflection of the city lights dancing across its surface like a warning.

And Claire.

Claire had secrets, too. He felt it, saw it flicker behind her eyes every time he got too close. But unlike Crystal's silence, Claire's distance didn't feel manipulative.

It felt scared.

Which made it worse.

He pushed away from the counter and stepped into the hallway, lights dimmed now, the buzz of energy finally drained from the penthouse. Somewhere down the corridor, he heard Camila laughing at a late-night show rerun, her voice sharp and unfiltered. A door clicked softly. The kids were moving, maybe brushing teeth, maybe plotting more paper towel fights.

And then he saw her.

Claire, leaning against the far wall, just outside her mother's room, arms folded over her chest, head tilted back. She didn't see him at first. Her eyes were closed, as if she were trying to breathe in calm.

Eric walked toward her quietly.

"Everyone settled?" he asked, his voice softer than he expected.

She startled, then smiled when she saw him. "More or less. Camila's found your fancy shampoo stash and declared it hers now. Olivia tried to convince Henry the guest toilet was haunted, so I'm guessing he'll hold it until sunrise."

Eric smirked. "Efficient use of fear. I respect it."

She sighed and pushed off the wall. "I was making sure Mom was okay. She doesn't always sleep well in new places."

There was a pause.

He stepped closer. Not too close.

"You didn't say much earlier," he said. "About Chloe."

Claire's shoulders tightened. "Because I don't know where she is."

"But you know *why*, don't you?" he asked gently.

Claire looked at him then. Her eyes weren't defensive, they were tired. Sad. But determined.

"I have ideas," she admitted. "But I'm not ready to share them."

Eric nodded. "Fair."

She studied him. "And you? Anything you're not ready to share?"

He gave a short, quiet laugh. "You'll need a longer night. Let's just say I understand what you are going through with your mom better than you know. My father died of something similar."

Claire frowned at that, faint and brief, then looked away. "I'm sorry for your loss. I lost my dad when I was a kid. It never gets easy."

The silence between them wasn't uncomfortable this time. It felt charged, humming with something unspoken but not unwelcome.

"I know you didn't ask for all this," she said finally, "but thank you. For letting us in. For not asking too many questions."

"I'm very good at pretending I have control," Eric said.

"Funny," she murmured, "so am I."

They stood there a moment longer, side by side in the quiet hallway, two people used to managing but unfamiliar with letting others see it.

Then: a crash from the kitchen.

Followed by Camila's voice: "ERIC, DO YOU HAVE A BROOM? DON'T ASK!"

Eric looked toward the noise and closed his eyes.

Claire covered a laugh with her hand. "I should go… supervise."

"I'll get the broom," he said, already turning.

"Alphabetized closet?"

"Don't insult me."

As she disappeared back into the madness, Eric lingered one last second.

He was in deeper than he'd planned.

And somehow, it no longer felt like a mistake.

* * *

Eric found Barry exactly where he expected him, on the balcony, still as a statue, tablet glowing in the dark, the city stretching out like a battlefield beneath them.

"You ever sleep?" Eric asked, stepping into the breeze.

Barry didn't glance up. "Sleep is for people with boring problems."

Eric leaned against the railing. "Got anything for me?"

Barry didn't look up from his screen, but the energy in the room shifted. "Two updates," he said. "First, Aidan just confirmed Crystal was spotted in Houston. Three days ago. Warehouse district, early morning. No entourage. In and out in under five minutes."

He finally looked up, voice tighter. "That's the first verified sighting since she left Cabo with the new boyfriend."

Eric's brow furrowed. "That's not normal behavior for her."

"Nope," Barry said. "Something's up. I've got eyes on the location. If she shows again, we'll know."

"And the sister?"

"Chloe's trickier. A traffic cam caught her outside Dallas, five-second flash, but it's her. She's staying mobile, using cash, burner phones if any. She's not running aimlessly."

Eric crossed his arms. "Then who's she hiding from?"

Barry paused. "Someone she's scared of."

That landed heavier than Eric liked.

Before he could respond, the doorbell rang.

Not a buzz. Not a knock. The *doorbell*, his very expensive, very unnecessary, custom-chimed doorbell, rang like a harpist had just entered the foyer.

Eric froze. "Please tell me that's not what I think it is."

Barry was already moving. "Stay here. I've got it."

Eric followed anyway.

When Barry opened the door, Gregory stood there, posture impeccable, face unreadable, but his eyes said everything: disdain, confusion, maybe a pinch of existential dread.

Behind him was a Supermart grocery cart, the kind with squeaky wheels and a half-busted brake, piled high with plastic bags and delivery totes.

"Mr. Whiff," Gregory said, voice flat, "a delivery. From… Supermart."

Eric blinked. "What in, ?"

The delivery kid, long hair and baggy pants, looked up from his phone. "Yo, you're Eric, right? Got, like, a bunch of bags here. Frozen stuff. Snacks. One bag is just fruit roll-ups. You got a party or something?"

Before Eric could speak, Camila came barreling around the corner like she'd heard the starter pistol at a sale.

"Oh, thank goodness," she said, rushing toward the cart. "That was faster than I expected!"

Eric stared. "Camila…"

She held up his American Express like a trophy. "Found this on the counter! Thought I'd do a quick order for the kids, nothing fancy. Just the essentials."

Barry's head turned. Slowly. "That's cartloads of groceries."

"They're *growing children*, Barry," she replied, already grabbing bags. "They eat like tornadoes."

"You used *my* card," Eric said flatly.

"I figured you wouldn't want Olivia eating olives stuffed with… more olives," she said, waving a jar. "Nothing is kid friendly. You can't expect all of us to live on the stuff you got here."

Barry stepped in front of the cart. "Camila. You can't just make purchases on someone's card without asking."

"Look, I even got stuff for you!" she protested, pulling out a bag of chips as her arms were full of boxed macaroni and cheese. "And technically, I was still on the premises. That's implied consent."

"No," Barry said. "It's not."

She huffed. "Okay, okay. I get it. I won't do it again. *Geez.* You people act like I ordered a pony."

Gregory cleared his throat. "Shall I alert the freight elevator next time?"

Eric gave him a tight smile. "I think… yes. Probably."

Camila was already hauling bags toward the kitchen. "Nathan! Pizza rolls! Olivia! I got the dinosaur ones!"

Barry slowly closed the door behind them, watching the cart's wobbly wheel veer left and slam into the baseboard.

Eric turned to him. "This is what losing control looks like."

Barry didn't miss a beat. "Better than being alone."

Eric shook his head, smiling despite himself.

And somewhere in the kitchen, Claire laughed.

Chapter 12

❧

Barry

Barry Poet knew havoc. He'd walked through war zones with nothing but a Kevlar vest and a black coffee. He'd stood between terrorists and kidnappers, diverted paparazzi with sleight-of-hand precision, and once neutralized a man with a fork at a black-tie gala in Dubai.

But this?

This was *domestic* turmoil.

As he stood in the living room of Eric Whiff's penthouse, watching the twins peel the plastic off a family-size pack of fruit roll-ups with gusto, Barry felt something he hadn't in years:

Mildly overwhelmed.

"Where do you want the cereal?" Camila shouted over her shoulder, already halfway into reorganizing Eric's pantry.

"Wherever it lands," Barry muttered, sipping a cup of Claire's iced brown sugar oat milk espresso with salted caramel foam. It was her usual, but now it was his too. The drink snuck into his life like poetry, quiet, underestimated, and suddenly essential.

Claire breezed past him, carrying a fresh towel for her mother who stayed in the bedroom closest to the living room. "Bathroom shelf, second door. I

111

labeled them."

Barry watched her go, steady and composed even as her world cracked at the edges. He admired that.

She didn't know it, but Barry increased security protocols. He'd changed the elevator codes, added facial recognition parameters, and disabled every external camera feed that could be traced. The penthouse was locked down tighter than a vault, and still, it didn't feel like enough.

He watched as Claire pushed Beatrice's wheelchair into the room and seated her near the window, letting her watch the skyline as if it were an old film she'd seen a hundred times. Her silence was louder than anything in the room.

"She likes to be here with the rest of us. All the action keeps her distracted," Claire shared as she went into the kitchen.

Eric sidled up beside him, sipping the same coffee. "So. How long until my espresso machine files for emancipation?"

"Depends," Barry said, "on how many Pop-Tarts Camila tries to toast at once."

Eric sighed. "I didn't sign up for this."

"Yes, you did," Barry said. "When you wrote your number on that napkin."

Eric said nothing. Just sipped. "I did sign us up for professional help, the nursing kind. She comes highly recommended and will be here this afternoon. It will help Claire and her family with Beatrice. Multiple Sclerosis is hard on any family."

Barry glanced at Eric in mild surprise. he saw a new side to the playboy—or former playboy, as it seemed.

"Have they said anything else about Chloe? I have not heard anything." Barry asked between sips of coffee.

Eric shook his head. "No. But she's the key to all of this. I can feel it."

Barry nodded. "I've got people watching traffic cams in every direction. She'll pop up again." Aidan and the rest of the team, in Mobile, used all major resources to find her and Crystal. Somehow, another part of a separate puzzle or a key to this one.

He didn't mention the ping he'd received that morning, a hit on a burner phone last used by Chloe Eidean near a freight stop outside Galveston. He hadn't told anyone yet. Not until he was sure.

Barry's phone vibrated. He pulled it out.

Unknown number.

He answered. "Poet."

Aidan's voice crackled through. "She left something behind. A bag."

Barry's spine straightened.

"What bag?"

"The girl. Claire's sister. She was at the old train yard. She left fast. Someone else was watching her. I grabbed what I could."

Barry's tone dropped. "Where are you?"

"Houston. Warehouse off Eldridge and Westheimer."

The line went dead.

Eric raised an eyebrow. "Problem?"

"Possible answer," Barry said. "I need an hour."

"Take all the time you need," Eric replied. "We'll be here. Loudly."

Barry set his coffee down. "Keep an eye on Claire."

Eric hesitated. "No problem. You think this is getting worse?"

Barry's voice was steel. "I think we're in the quiet before the gunfire."

He turned, grabbed his jacket, and slipped the pistol into his holster. Then, almost as an afterthought, he returned to the coffee, lifted the cup, and drained it.

And with that, Barry stepped into the elevator, the door closing behind him with a soft, final *ding*.

* * *

The warehouse at the corner of Eldridge and Westheimer experienced better decades. Its rusted rooflines sagged like weary shoulders, and the overhead lights buzzed with the dying pulse of old sodium filaments.

Barry Poet didn't need the map; he'd been here before, long ago, for something far worse. Places like this attracted the worst elements in people like a moth to a flame. It was a former human trafficking stop, busted by the FBI years ago. He tracked a client to this location.

He parked the black SUV four blocks out and down a dark alley. Walked the rest. Silent. Armed. The city never really slept, but this part of town had slipped into something more feral. A possum darted under a chain-link fence. A flickering neon "Open" sign blinked from a taco stand that hadn't been open in years.

Barry reached the door.

A single knock. Then a pause. Then two more.

The door creaked open.

Aidan stood inside, a youthful energy despite the shadows. He had that look of a person who could fix anything on the fly. The ability to blend into and be accepted in challenging situations was why Barry hired him in the first place.

"Poet," he whispered.

Barry stepped in. "Talk."

Aidan gestured toward a rust-stained table in the back. A duffel bag sat there, old, navy blue, with a zipper that had seen war. Barry moved to it, flipped it open.

Inside:

A pack of cigarettes.

A burner phone, wrapped in a rubber band.

Two folded shirts, still damp.

And at the very bottom…a worn, leather-bound journal.

Barry picked it up slowly. The initials on the front were burned into the corner:

C.Eidean

He opened it.

At first glance, the handwriting appeared rough, looped, rushed, yet methodical. Pages filled with half-coded notes, dates, names.

One stuck out.

March 8 – If I disappear, start with the man in the green truck. He always parks facing out. He doesn't blink when I look at him.

Barry flipped another page.

Don't trust the woman at the shelter with red hair. She asks too many questions, she already knows the answers to.

And then another.

If Camila or Claire find this, I'm sorry. I was trying to keep the danger from spreading. But it already has.

Barry closed the journal slowly. "Where did you find it?"

Aidan shrugged. "She dropped the bag behind a crate. Didn't even look back. But I saw another guy, tall, maybe military. Watching her. Didn't approach. Just… waited. He didn't follow her when she ran."

Barry's instincts sharpened. "He wasn't trying to catch her."

"Nope."

"He was trying to see where she'd go."

"Yep."

Barry pocketed the phone, zipped the journal inside his coat. He looked at Aidan. "You didn't see me tonight."

Aidan gave a lopsided smile. "I never do."

Barry stepped back into the night.

He was already dialing by the time he hit the sidewalk.

"Eric," he said when the line picked up. "We've got confirmation. Chloe's alive. But she's not hiding from danger. She's dancing with it."

Eric exhaled. "Did you discover anything?"

"Goldmine. A backpack and a journal. She knew what she was doing. And someone's been watching her longer than we thought."

"Do we tell Claire?"

Barry paused. A siren wailed in the distance.

"Not yet. I need more. I want names, faces, and timelines." He glanced back at the building. "This is just the first breadcrumb."

Eric was quiet for a beat. Then: "Come back safe."

Barry smirked. "It's me."

He ended the call, adjusted the weight of the backpack and its contents, and stepped into the shadows.

There was a ghost in Houston, and Barry was going to catch it before it burned the whole family alive.

** * **

Barry Poet stepped off the private elevator and immediately regretted not giving himself another ten minutes to mentally prepare. The moment the doors slid open, a blur in footed pajamas darted across the marble foyer with a primal squeal. Something about cereal and "jail for marshmallow crimes."

He'd survived ambushes in Kabul that were quieter than this.

He slipped inside, closing the door with a soft click, and paused to scan the penthouse. Camila was in the kitchen, elbows deep in what looked like a self-assembled cheese-based art project. Claire's voice floated in from the guest wing, sharp and urgent.

Then he heard it:

"Barry!"

He turned. Claire stood in the hallway, holding something tight against her chest. Eric was beside her, his expression grim.

Barry crossed the room fast. "What is it?"

Claire handed it to him without a word. It looked like the journal in the backpack. He unzipped it and reached inside to be sure it was still there. It was, so what was this?

He took the leather-bound book in his hands, flipping it open. The handwriting was unmistakable, looped, familiar, laced with desperation. Chloe's. Just like the journal he already had from the warehouse.

He skimmed a few pages. *Green truck. No blinking. Woman at the shelter. March 8th.* All the same phrases. Same voice.

Eric's voice was low beside him. "Claire found it in her suitcase. Hidden in a duffle bag. Chloe must've tucked it there the last time she visited."

Claire nodded. "We were in such a rush to leave, I didn't even notice it until we got here. I meant to look through it, but it's confusing. Disjointed. It doesn't make much sense yet."

Claire looked down. "I didn't mean to keep it a secret. I wasn't sure what it meant. I needed time to figure it out before bringing it to everyone. The things Chloe wrote, it's like a puzzle with missing pieces. And I didn't want to raise alarms unless I knew it was real."

Barry felt the electric crack of his instincts snapping into place. "She planted this. Meant for someone to find it. But not right away."

Claire nodded. "She was trying to protect us. But she knew it wouldn't hold."

Barry flipped further until he hit the last entry.

"If they find me, they'll try to get to Claire next. I left the name. It's in the list. The rest, I'm sorry."

He closed the journal slowly, like sealing a vault.

"I just left a warehouse in west Houston, burned-out place. Guy handed me a bag Chloe dropped. This journal wasn't in it. She must've had a second one. She's covering her tracks."

Claire paled. "So someone else is looking for her."

"Worse," Barry said. "They're letting her run, to see who she leads them to."

Eric looked toward the bedroom where Beatrice slept. "You think they're watching us?"

Barry was already moving. He crossed to the panel in the wall, fingers flying across the digital lock. Security screens flickered to life, showing night vision feeds from interior cameras. "They can't see *in.* But that doesn't mean they're not near."

He turned to Claire. "These journals change everything. It's not only about Chloe running, this is about someone wanting to disappear *her* and anyone tied to her."

Claire's voice was steady, but barely. "What do we do?"

Barry looked at her. Not the woman from TruePair. Not the academic with clever eyes and Post-it note precision. The sister. The daughter. The one left behind, now standing in the center of a very real battlefield.

"We take the next step," he said. "Carefully."

Eric raised an eyebrow. "Which is?"

Barry tapped the front cover of one of the journals.

"We find the green truck."

Then he looked at Claire again.

"And this time, we do it *my* way."

* * *

Barry sat alone at the oversized kitchen island, elbows resting on polished marble, Chloe Eidean's two journals laid open before him. One with a worn leather cover, edges frayed from use, the other newer with a stiff spine and pages ready to be broken in.

Chloe's notes were a hurried mix of detailed explanations and travels. As he skimmed through the pages he noted her time spent in recovery and the struggle to get her life back on track. He admired her for taking those hard steps.

She also detailed her time in the homeless shelter and the woman she met there. Mixed in with her struggles and observations, he noticed the uptick in paranoia and concern about someone following her. She was helping the woman work with children in the shelter until something changed. Here was where the green truck first appeared in her notes.

Barry looked up from the journals and realized that the rest of the penthouse was finally quiet. Even the cat had gone still, curled like an elegant judgment near the foot of Eric's leather recliner.

Barry didn't sleep on nights like this.

He studied the entry again, the one circled twice in smudged blue ink:

"He never blinks. Always backs in. Green truck. Same abandoned gas station off I-10 and Wycliffe. Tuesday nights. 9:30 p.m."

He had already sent the note to Aidan and his team. One would grab camera security footage. Another was scanning traffic cams for any truck matching the vague make and model he'd built from memory. The work was moving. What kept Barry rooted was the implication.

Chloe hadn't run blindly. She'd *planned.*

She'd observed someone and decided not to report him, but to *write him down.* That took fear. That took knowledge. And that took time.

Barry flipped another page. More paranoia. More patterns. A list of phone numbers. A map sketched in the margin of a half-torn sheet. None of it added up yet.

A soft rustle behind him.

Claire entered the kitchen barefoot, her hair pulled up in a messy knot, wearing a hoodie and cradling two mugs. She offered him one.

"You're still up," she said.

"I don't sleep much when things are shifting," Barry replied, accepting the mug. He sipped. The drink was her usual, of course, *his* usual now, too. It had become a kind of truce between them it was a ritual.

Claire settled into the stool across from him. Her voice was quiet. "What aren't you telling me?"

Barry studied her for a long time. She didn't blink. Just like Chloe's green truck. Good. She was stronger than she thought.

"I think your sister's playing a longer game than we realized," he said. "And we're not the only ones following the trail she left."

Claire swallowed. "You think she's bait."

"I think she *made herself* bait to protect you. But it's starting to backfire."

Claire closed her eyes. "She should've told me."

"She didn't want you to have to choose," Barry said. "That's what this kind of thing does. Makes people draw lines. Burn bridges."

Claire leaned forward, glancing at the journals. "You've seen this before, haven't you? Not just the pattern. The sacrifice."

Barry didn't answer right away. He flipped the journals closed and met her gaze.

"I've seen people run to save their family. I've seen what it costs them."

Claire's voice was raw. "Will she make it?"

Barry hesitated. "If we move fast. And smart."

She looked down at her hands. "Then tell me what to do."

That stopped him.

She wasn't asking to be protected anymore. She was asking to be part of the solution.

Barry pushed the journals toward her. "Learn them. Every page. Memorize her patterns. We're not looking for where she is. We're looking for where she *means* to go. What she wants to say without revealing it."

Claire nodded. No fear now. Just resolve.

Barry stood, grabbing his coat. "I'll be back by sunrise. I'm going to check a few places. I want to see who else has been watching." Barry was going to meet up with Aidan and his team via Zoom call, but she didn't need to know this. He suspected the FBI might want to know about what Chloe was involved in.

Claire's voice followed him as he reached the elevator.

"You trust me now?"

Barry turned, giving her a look that was part respect, part warning. "I trusted you the moment you handed me that coffee."

He hit the button.

"And I'll trust you more when you don't blink."

The elevator doors closed with a whisper.

Barry was hunting a green truck.

But more than that, he was placing a quiet, calculated bet on Claire Eidean.

Chapter 13

Claire

Claire slipped down the hallway; Chloe's two journals clutched to her chest like contraband. The penthouse buzzed with muffled noises as everyone started to get up, cartoons on the living room TV, Camila clinking through the kitchen, the occasional shriek of "He took my sock!" echoing from one of the guest rooms.

She needed quiet. Order.

The library called to her.

She pushed open the double doors and stepped into stillness. The scent of leather bindings and aged paper greeted her like an old friend. Floor-to-ceiling bookshelves wrapped the walls, each one meticulously arranged by genre and author. She half-smiled. Of course, Eric alphabetized by surname. The man probably slept in color-coded pajamas, a sight a part of her didn't mind seeing.

But as her gaze traveled, she saw more than order. She saw reverence. The antique globe in the corner, sun-faded and scuffed, bore the careful marks of restoration. A brass telescope, likely 19th century, rested near the windows, its polished surface gleaming despite the filtered light. And then, the books. Not just first editions, but pieces of history. A leather-bound *Don*

Quixote from 1821. A weathered 1859 copy of *On the Origin of Species.* An 1870 reprint of *Leaves of Grass,* edges foxed, cover embossed with vines, and tucked behind a glass case near the fireplace, a signed first edition of *The Great Gatsby.*

She ran her fingers along the spines. She found herself hoping Eric looked at any other thing else in his life with that same quiet devotion.

She crossed to the long walnut reading table near the back, settled into a chair, and opened the first journal.

Chloe's handwriting hit like a series of messy loops, all caps in places, and occasionally water-smudged ink. Names. Dates. A few crude sketches, her life in rehab, and a homeless shelter. Claire pulled her knees to her chest and leaned over the pages, completely absorbed.

A green truck again. Dent shaped like a crescent moon.

The woman at the shelter.

Don't trust her.

She flipped to the second journal, the newer one. This one was more frantic. A line circled so many times, the page now worn thin:

March 8 – If I disappear, start with the man in the green truck. Dent.

Claire's pen hovered over a sticky note. Her mind whirled, pulling together fragments of Chloe's cryptic trail. It wasn't random. It was intentional. Chloe was trying to lead them somewhere.

She didn't hear Eric enter.

"Didn't mean to interrupt," he said gently.

Claire jumped slightly, then looked up. He stood just inside the door, coffee in hand, his sleeves rolled up, his expression open.

She noticed the way the morning light caught his jawline's edge, casting soft shadows and emphasizing the sharp angles of his face. The rolled sleeves revealed strong forearms, dusted lightly with hair, he looked less like the curated billionaire from glossy profiles and more like someone on the street. Tangible. And, if she let herself admit it, annoyingly attractive.

"I thought you'd be in the office," he added. "However, this is more your space."

His voice was casual, but his eyes lingered on her a moment longer than necessary. She felt a flicker of heat rise, one that had nothing to do with the coffee in his hand.

Claire gave a quick nod, then glanced down at the journals. "I needed a place where I could breathe."

He walked over and set the coffee down beside her. "Mind if I join you?"

She hesitated, just long enough for him to notice, then slid the second journal a few inches toward him in silent invitation.

He pulled out a chair and sat beside her, their movements unconsciously syncing. For a while, neither of them spoke. They read in tandem, the silence between them soft and companionable. Their shoulders brushed occasionally, each time lingering just a little longer. Once, when they both leaned in to decipher a smudged line, their faces were so close she could feel the warmth of his breath near her cheek. She didn't pull away.

It surprised her how natural it felt, this shared quiet, this closeness, as though they were partners in something that mattered. Like maybe, despite everything, they were becoming something more.

Claire pointed at a line. "That's the third time she mentions a Tuesday night."

Eric nodded. "And always at the same location, somewhere off I-10. It's a pattern."

"She left this for us," Claire said softly. "I think she knew someone would find it eventually. It's the reason she made two journals; in case she lost one, there was another to be found."

Eric turned toward her. "You're incredible, you know that?"

Claire blinked. "What?"

"Most people would be curled up in a ball after the last few days. You're here. Parsing information like you're solving a puzzle only you can finish."

She gave a dry laugh. "Maybe that's just the librarian in me. Sorting facts into something legible."

Eric's smile was faint. "Or maybe you're just braver than you think."

Their eyes met.

Claire's heart stuttered. The air shifted, charged with something electric but delicate.

"I've been trying to figure you out since the auction," she admitted, her voice just above a whisper. "And then with Ethan… I didn't know what was real anymore. The names, the walls, we were both hiding."

Eric's gaze didn't leave hers. "I didn't either," he said, his voice low and steady, carrying more weight than volume. "But this," He gestured between them, to the books, the journals, the quiet rhythm they had somehow fallen into. "This feels real."

She followed the motion of his hand and then looked back at him. "Because it's not about the profiles or the pretense. There's no algorithm here."

"No," he said, his smile softening. "Just you, me, and two old journals full of heartbreak and breadcrumbs."

She laughed gently, tension slipping out of her shoulders. "Trust you to call my sister's trauma a breadcrumb trail."

"I meant it with affection," he replied, nudging her knee beneath the table, the contact warm and intentional. "But if it helps, I think you're the same. Complex. Guarded. But quietly extraordinary."

"Careful," she murmured, tilting her head, "I might take that as flirting."

He leaned in slightly, his voice a murmur just for her. "What if it is?"

The pause that followed wasn't awkward. It pulsed with the ache of possibility—something fragile, something just beginning to bloom.

She didn't reply. Not with words.

Instead, she leaned in.

Their lips met, tentative at first, barely a question. Then again, slower, a little braver. Claire's hand rested lightly against his chest. Eric's fingers found the edge of the journal she held, brushing hers.

It wasn't a perfect kiss.

But it felt honest.

When they parted, neither moved right away.

Claire exhaled, steadying her voice. "We should probably keep going."

Eric nodded. "Yeah. Before the twins decide how far the cat can fly across the couch again."

Claire smiled, pulling the journal closer. "Back to the trail then."

But as they returned to the pages, something had shifted.

Between all the fear and the questions, they were two people in a quiet library, decoding a sister's secrets, and, maybe, beginning something of their own.

\#

The journal lay open, Chloe's hurried script snaking across the page. Claire tried to stay focused, but the words blurred, her thoughts drifting back to the kiss. Not because she wanted them to. Because they *wouldn't stop*.

It had caught her off guard.

Not the fact that Eric kissed her, she'd seen the tension building between them, felt the air shift every time he stood too close or said something quietly kind. No, what surprised her was *how* he kissed her.

It was confident. Measured. The kind of kiss someone gave when noy trying to impress, only to connect.

Sam never kissed her like that.

With Sam, there was always a hint of detachment. His kisses were soft, polite, almost clinical, as though he were checking a box on the intimacy checklist. Sweet, sure. But always reserved. Always distracted.

Eric kissed her like she was the only thing tethering him to earth.

And worse?

She liked it.

Claire forced her attention back to the journal and underlined a half-coded phrase about someone getting in the green truck. But the warmth on her lips remained along with the memory of his hand gently brushing her cheek, like she might vanish should he move too fast. Eric Whiff was experienced; there was no denying it. But instead of intimidating her, it made her curious.

Maybe experience wasn't a red flag. Maybe it was a sign he understood what mattered.

Her pen stilled.

Then,

"CLAIRE!"

The library doors slammed open with the force of a family emergency. Claire flinched, nearly knocking her coffee off the table. Eric's chair scraped the floor as he jolted beside her, almost flipping it backwards. He grabbed her arm to stay upright.

Camila stood framed in the doorway, eyes blazing and clearly mid-rant.

Claire braced. "What now?"

Camila stormed into the room, arms slicing the air as she spoke. "Your *son* is eating marshmallows out of the bag. Like an actual gremlin. Those were for hot chocolate later today not your cat."

Claire blinked. "My… wait, Oliver?"

"YES. Your cat. The four-legged con artist with boundary issues."

Claire sighed, dragging a hand down her face. "He opened the pantry?"

"He *unlocked* the childproof latch. Climbed in. Ripped open a bag of rainbow marshmallows with his *teeth* and is now sitting on top of a box of granola like some feline warlord. And when I tried to stop him? He growled at me. Growled."

Eric choked back a laugh. Claire didn't even look at him.

"I told you not to store snacks near the countertop," she muttered, standing. "He sees it as an invitation."

Camila threw her hands up. "Well, he's accepted. And now he's hosting a private tea party with refined sugar."

Claire started toward the door.

"I'll get him."

"You might want to bring a laser pointer and a bribe," Camila called after her. "He's guarding the marshmallows like national treasure."

Claire paused, turned slightly, and glanced at Eric.

She hadn't meant to say it, but the words came anyway.

"I haven't kissed anyone since Sam, my ex-boyfriend."

He straightened slightly, caught off guard.

"And?" he asked, quiet but not casual.

Claire's mouth lifted, just enough.

"Yours was better. We might have to study it again."

Then she turned and left the library, trying not to overthink the way her heart kicked up as she walked. Or the fact that Oliver was probably licking dye off his paws while plotting the next pantry heist.

Behind her, she heard Eric exhale slow and steady, but it carried a weight she felt between her shoulder blades.

From the hallway came the unmistakable sound of rustling bags and a victorious meow.

Claire quickened her pace.

"Oliver!" she called. "Give me the bag this instant!"

The only response was the soft thud of another box hitting the floor.

She rolled her eyes as she rounded the corner.

This life wasn't the one she imagined.

But standing between journals with clues, a man with better kisses than he had any right to, and a marshmallow-thieving cat?

She was okay with it.

\#

By the time Claire coaxed Oliver down from the pantry shelf, half-purring, half-pouting, a few pastel marshmallows still stuck to his whiskers, she was sweating, mildly sticky, and two steps from Googling feline boarding schools. She returned to the library with a hair tie in her mouth and a trail of rainbow sugar dust on her shirt.

Eric didn't look up right away.

He was still seated at the long table, elbows braced on either side of Chloe's journal. His expression had shifted to a focused, intense, and thoughtful one. The room was quieter than she'd left it. Almost reverent.

Claire paused in the doorway, watching him.

There was something about the way he leaned in, brow furrowed, fingers unconsciously tracing the edge of the paper, that caught her off guard. Not just his posture, but also his presence, rooted, steady. She hadn't seen him like this before. No bravado. No guarded charm. Just a man trying to understand something bigger than himself.

And it struck her then, Eric Whiff, billionaire tech disruptor, was sitting in silence, wholly absorbed in the fragmented words of her sister's pain. Not because it served him. But because he cared.

It was unexpected. Disarming.

Beautiful.

Claire paused in the doorway. "Please tell me you didn't find a cat manifesto in there."

Eric didn't smile.

He tapped a page instead. "I think I found a location."

Claire crossed the room, her amusement gone. "Show me."

He turned the journal toward her.

"Look here," he said, pointing to a page she hadn't reached yet. The writing was more frantic than the earlier entries, shaky, slightly smeared as if written in a hurry. "She wrote this on a different kind of paper. See how the ink bled? It's a receipt page, torn from the back of something. And this," he tapped a jagged circle near the bottom, "isn't a drawing."

Claire leaned in.

The circle was messy, like someone had tried to sketch in the dark. But inside it was three oddly familiar letters.

"M.E.C.?" she read aloud. "Is that a company?"

Eric shook his head. "That's the Midtown Energy Co-op. An old utility site shut down years ago. They used to store maintenance records in an office off Wycliffe and I-10."

Claire's eyes widened. "That's the same intersection Chloe mentioned. Repeatedly."

Eric nodded. "Exactly. I thought it was an abandoned gas station on Google Street view, but maybe not. The journal keeps circling back to that area."

Claire took the journal and flipped through the surrounding pages. Now that she knew what to look for, it was all over the margins: *Green truck parked facing out. Tuesdays. Same gas station. No lights after midnight.* A line on the page, then beside it in another group, ten lines, then a break, and three more.

"She was watching someone," Claire murmured. "Or something. Repeated visits. She must've been trying to map their routine."

Eric's tone was careful. "This looks like surveillance."

Claire swallowed. "You think she was following them?"

"I think she was trying to prove something. Or intercept something. She knew she was in danger, but she didn't run. She documented it instead."

Claire sat down beside him, a familiar mix of dread and admiration growing in her chest. "Classic Chloe. Brave and reckless and always one step ahead, until she's not."

Eric gently turned another page. "Look at this, 'if Claire finds this, I didn't tell you because I thought I could stop it first. But if you're reading this, I couldn't.'"

Claire's breath caught. "She wrote that to me?"

Eric met her gaze. "Looks like it."

Claire's fingers gripped the edge of the page. She blinked hard, once, then again.

Eric let the silence settle a moment before speaking.

"I want to go there," he said. "Tomorrow. I know Barry's already working the angles, but if Chloe left this breadcrumb for *you*, maybe it's time we follow it."

Claire didn't answer right away.

Her instinct said no. That this was dangerous, possibly reckless.

But then she looked down at the journal in her hand, at her sister's handwriting, looping and urgent and deeply personal, and something steadied inside her.

"We're not going without backup," she said firmly. "And if Barry says it's too hot, we wait. But we *go*. She wanted us to. She *needs* us to."

Eric nodded once, serious.

Claire glanced back at the pages.

She didn't know what was waiting for them at the gas station across from Midtown Energy Co-op.

But it was no longer just about Chloe running.

It was about what she'd found.

And what she hadn't had time to tell.

\#

Claire knocked on the guest suite door with two sharp taps. No answer.

She tried again, then turned the knob.

The day had dragged in that strange way time moves when you're waiting for something you can't control. Barry left early that morning with little more than a nod and a promise to "check a few things." He hadn't returned, and with every hour that passed, the silence grew heavier.

Eric had spent most of the afternoon in his office, the door slightly ajar—a quiet signal that he was occupied but present. Claire, left to the rest of the penthouse, found herself wandering more than she meant to.

It was like stepping through someone else's curated museum, minimalist lines, thoughtful art, shelves of old books and modern philosophy. Everything in its place. Or it had been.

Now, the sleek kitchen counter was cluttered with her niece's markers and a half-eaten box of cereal. A stuffed unicorn had taken up residence on the designer sofa. One of her mother's pill organizers sat next to a framed photo of Eric with some high-profile tech award. And her sister's oversized tote was inexplicably draped over a Danish leather chair that did not deserve abuse.

Eric's world, polished, quiet, precise, was no longer his own. And yet he hadn't said a word about the mess.

She wasn't sure what that meant. But she noticed.

Barry returned later that evening, slipping in with barely a word. His expression was unreadable, his usual steady presence weighed down by something heavier. He nodded once at Eric, gave Claire the faintest glance, and then disappeared down the hall to his private suite.

She waited until the apartment quieted—until Camila stopped pacing and the kids finally slept, until the city outside dimmed beneath the dusk.

Then Claire crossed the hall and raised her hand.

She knocked on Barry's door.

Once. Then again.

This time, she didn't wait for permission to speak.

"Barry," she said softly, "I think we need to talk."

Barry was awake, of course. He returned a few hours earlier from the errand he ran. He sat at the small desk near the window, scrolling through satellite images on his tablet, a mug of black coffee beside him, steam curling into the dim light.

"You don't sleep, do you?" Claire asked.

Barry didn't look up. "Only when no one needs protecting. So, no."

Eric stepped in behind her, holding Chloe's journals like they were made of glass.

Barry finally glanced over, and when he saw the journal, he set the tablet aside.

"What happened?"

Claire handed him the book. "We found something. A location."

Barry took it, flipping to the marked page with practiced efficiency. His eyes flicked over the sketch, the lettering, the scribbled coordinates.

"M.E.C.," he read aloud. "Midtown Energy Co-op. Decommissioned site. You're right, it's near Wycliffe and I-10. Not exactly a tourist destination."

"She circled back to that intersection multiple times," Eric said. "There's something there at the gas station. Something she didn't have time to explain."

Barry leaned back, nodding slowly. "Could be a dead drop. Could be a meeting point. Could be nothing."

"But she took the risk," Claire said. "Whatever's there, she thought it was worth documenting. And she wanted me to find it."

Barry's gaze locked onto hers. "And now you want to go."

Claire didn't flinch. "Yes."

A long pause. Barry set the journal down gently. "Then we do it carefully. No improvisation. No hero speeches. We go at dawn. I'll scout it first."

Eric crossed his arms. "I'm coming."

"You're not trained for recon," Barry said flatly.

"I'm not going to sit here and wait while you disappear into danger with Claire. If she's going, I'm going."

Barry stared at him. Then sighed. "Fine. But you stay in the car until I give the all-clear."

Claire expected Eric to argue, but he simply nodded.

Barry stood, already shifting into field mode. "I'll prep the gear. You two rest. This adventure isn't an amateur hour."

He picked up the journal again, studying the lines and loops of Chloe's handwriting. "She was smart. And scared."

"She's still out there," Claire said. "I know it."

Barry didn't argue.

He walked to his closet and opened a duffel bag. He then began to lay out the contents which included a flashlight, comm earpieces, a secondary phone, a compact first aid kit.

Then, as if to himself, he murmured:

"The truth walks veiled through wire and rust,

And waits for those who still dare trust."

Claire blinked. "That one yours?"

Barry didn't look up. "Yeah."

Eric leaned toward Claire and whispered, "He has a poem for every situation."

"Good," she whispered back. "Because we're walking into one."

Barry strapped on a shoulder holster. "Be ready in five hours. I want to be in and out before the city wakes up."

Claire nodded.

They left the room in silence, the weight of the next step pressing down like a storm on the horizon.

She didn't know what they'd find at the co-op.

But tomorrow, they would walk into the unknown. Together.

Chapter 14

Eric

By 9 a.m., Eric's penthouse had officially become unrecognizable. The living room looked like a toy catalog exploded. There were glitter stickers on his espresso machine, and Chloe's journals were spread across the coffee table beside a stuffed llama wearing someone's scarf. Oliver the cat had taken up a perch atop the liquor cabinet, tail flicking like a judge deliberating everyone's sentence.

Still, amid the absurdity, it was Claire who kept everything from tilting unmanageably. When the registered nurse arrived this morning to care for Beatrice, Eric saw relief in her eyes. Camilia responded a little differently. She hooped for joy and danced all around the living room and kitchen singing, "Moving On Up to the Eastside…"

Claire touched Eric's arm and he felt it tingle. "Thank you so much, and I am sorry about my sister. I will talk with her. We will pay you back for everything."

Eric smiled at her, "Sometimes we need to do things to help each other out. Especially if you care about them." The way her eyes met his at that moment, he forgot time.

Now she sat cross-legged on the sofa, Chloe's handwriting under her fingertips, a pencil between her teeth, glasses slipping down her nose. Her hair was pulled into a lazy knot, and her coffee, brown sugar oat milk espresso with salted caramel foam went untouched.

Eric stood in the kitchen, watching her, pretending he wasn't memorizing every inch.

Then the elevator chimed.

Camila's voice rang out before she was even fully in the room. "He's here!"

Claire looked up. "Who?"

A duffel bag chunked against the wall, and then in strolled Charles, fully dressed in a vintage Star Trek science officer uniform, complete with communicator, boots, and smugness.

Claire's face flattened. "Seriously? How many outfits does he have?"

Charles beamed. "Came straight from GalaxieCon. You wouldn't believe the panel on warp-field inconsistencies. Camila filled me in and Barry met me downstairs. This place is better than the Ready Room!"

Eric blinked. "Spock's here to save the day?"

Barry, appearing from the hallway, muttered, "Only if the day involves snacks and delusion. The doorman took one look at him and walked away."

Camila flounced in behind him, oblivious. "I figured it was time for the whole family to be together again. Hi, Love." She greeted her husband with a kiss.

Claire looked like she might explode.

Eric held up a hand before she could. "Enough. I'm moving your entire circus one floor down."

Camila blinked. "Wait. What?"

"I bought the apartment under this one years ago," Eric said, typing a code into the wall panel. "It's furnished. Private. Quiet. And for now, it's yours."

Camila opened her mouth, probably to thank him extravagantly or ask if it had heated towel racks, but Claire stepped in fast.

"It's temporary," she warned, voice hard. "You respect the space. You respect this man. You do not turn it into a spa slash daycare slash delivery hub."

Camila huffed but nodded.

Barry added, "I'll escort the Starfleet officers downstairs and reset security on both floors."

Eric turned to Claire. "You're staying here."

She hesitated. "But…"

"You're safer upstairs. Chloe's journal had your name. I want you where Barry and I can see you."

Claire met his gaze. Slowly nodded. He could see the slight tilt of a smile on her face.

Camilia piped up, "Yes, Claire. Stay up here and get to know Eric. This family needs his cash, I mean, help."

"And my mom?" she asked.

"The registered nurse is permanent in-home care. There is a handicap bathroom downstairs, so it's better for Beatrice. She deserves comfort, not cartoons," Eric pointed out.

Claire exhaled. "Thank you."

"You don't have to thank me."

But she did anyway, with her eyes, with the way her shoulders finally dropped an inch.

As Camila and Charles herded the kids toward the elevator, Charles called back, "I call the room with the mirror. It has the best warp-lighting for TikToks."

Eric closed his eyes. "Beam me up, Scotty."

An hour later, the quiet settled like fresh snow.

Claire returned to the living room, arms folded, hair a little messier, but her expression clearer. Oliver trailed behind her, jumped up onto the couch, and immediately began making biscuits on Eric's throw blanket.

"They're settled." she said.

Eric nodded. "And you're here. Where I want you."

She arched a brow. "That a line?"

"Not yet. I'm working on it."

She laughed softly, walking to the window. "I didn't expect any of this."

"Me neither."

Eric joined her. She looked out over the city, the skyline sharp against the pale sky. The light made her hair glow.

"Claire," he said gently, "you're not a burden."

She looked over at him, guarded. "Feels like I am."

"You're not. You're the only thing about this that feels right."

He reached out and brushed her fingers.

She didn't pull away.

Before he could say more, his phone buzzed.

$89.65 – Supermart FeastFlex.

Eric frowned. "Oh, come on."

Claire glanced over. "What?"

"My card. Camila just ordered a second round of snacks. Ten 'Gummy Volcano Surprises' and something called 'CheesyBlasters XL.'"

Claire groaned. "I told her not to."

"It's fine." He tapped a few buttons. "Card is locked now."

She winced. "I'll go down there and explain."

He stopped her. "Let it go. Honestly, locking her out of my accounts was the most satisfying thing I've done all day. She's rather cheap compared to some of the ex-girlfriends."

Oliver meowed, as if in agreement.

Then, another buzz from a text, this time from Barry.

2:00 p.m. – Co-op site is clear. SUV ready. Move in sixty.

Eric looked at Claire. "We leave in an hour."

She nodded. "I'll get my gear."

She turned to go but paused. Looked at him.

"I'm glad I'm still up here," she said.

He stepped closer. "I don't want you anywhere else."

Their eyes locked.

No interruptions. No glitter. No overcooked Gummy Volcanoes.

Just breath.

Then, softly, carefully, she leaned in and kissed him.

Short. Grounded. Real.

"I'll meet you at the front door," she whispered.

And just like that, she was gone.

Eric stood there a moment, stunned in the best way.

Oliver headbutted his ankle, as if to say, "bout time."

* * *

By the time they pulled out of the underground garage, the sun had started its slow drop toward the west. The heat had softened into a dull shimmer along the pavement, and Eric's SUV cut through traffic like it had a mission.

Because it did.

Barry drove, as always, calm, unreadable, and tuned into half a dozen frequencies only he could hear. He hadn't said much beyond the necessary: "Site was quiet. Two access points. One surveillance blind spot. Bring flashlights."

Eric sat beside Claire in the backseat, eyes on the passing city, Chloe's journals clutched in her lap like a talisman. She hadn't spoken since they left. But she didn't need to.

Eric could feel the pressure building in her, the tension of hope laced with fear. He was terrified of what they might find. Or worse, what they might not.

He reached over and gently rested his hand on hers.

She didn't flinch. Just turned her palm up, laced their fingers together, and kept staring out the window.

No words.

Just that connection.

He let her be.

The car hummed along I-10, then took an abrupt exit onto a road that looked like the city had forgotten it years ago. Cracked asphalt. Faded signage. The skyline dropped behind them, swallowed by low industrial buildings and crooked fences.

They pulled into a gravel lot next to the only gas station in the area. Rusted fencing surrounded overgrown weeds. Ahead stood the remains of the Midtown Energy Co-op, low brick buildings, boarded windows, and a collapsing loading dock. The place looked abandoned in mid-thought.

Claire's voice was quiet but steady. "This is it."

Barry cut the engine. The silence that followed was deafening.

"Two of my people swept it this morning," Barry said. "No activity. No cameras. No movement. But it's too quiet. Someone's keeping it that way."

Eric opened his door. The heat hit him immediately, stale and stagnant. He stepped out and scanned the area. There were no cars. No power lines humming. No wind. Just silence and that eerie stillness that said someone might be watching.

Claire climbed out after him, laying the journals on the seat before closing the car door.

Barry handed her a flashlight. "The only remnants out here now are the old gas pumps and that maintenance building. That one."

He pointed to the far-left structure, smaller than the rest, half-swallowed by shadows and a leaning chain-link fence.

Eric stepped up beside Claire. "You ready?"

She exhaled slowly. "No. But we go anyway."

Barry gave a short nod. "I'll take point."

They moved as one, Barry ahead, Eric and Claire close behind. Gravel crunched underfoot, the sound jarringly loud in the quiet. Eric kept his hand near Claire's elbow—not because she needed steadying, but they were doing this together.

Barry reached the door first. He tested the handle, locked. With a practiced motion, he knelt, pulled a slim tool from his jacket, and had the rusted latch popped in seconds.

Claire arched a brow. "Is that in the official bodyguard handbook?"

Barry didn't look up. "Chapter seven: breaking and entering with grace."

Eric smirked, but the humor vanished the moment the door creaked open.

The smell hit them first: mold, rusted metal, and decay. Dust billowed in thick clouds as Claire swept her flashlight across the crumbling interior. Rows of rust-streaked filing cabinets loomed like forgotten sentinels. Fixtures dangled at odd angles. Cobwebs glinted like silent warnings.

They moved carefully, weaving between the rows.

Claire paused, reaching for the nearest drawer. It groaned open with a screech that

echoed down the corridor. Inside: old maintenance records, brittle and yellowed, listing inspection dates, wiring blueprints, meter readings.

But further back, tucked between two file folders, she pulled out a thick envelope

labeled in faint black ink:

Personnel Transfers – MEC Pickup Logs

Barry moved in beside her. "What the hell is that?"

Claire opened the envelope. Inside were dozens of forms, each listing names—first and last—alongside dates, codes, and destinations.

Eric frowned. "Midtown Energy Co-op. These look like transit records."

Claire turned one over. "Except this doesn't read like utility business. Look—these names, a few are marked with an 'X' and rerouted through El Paso… and some of them I've seen before. On Chloe's list."

Barry stepped closer, scanning the documents. "Someone's been using the defunct co-op as a cover. These aren't employees, they're people. People being moved."

Claire's hands tightened around the paper. "She was right. She wasn't imagining it. They're moving people not equipment."

Eric reached for one of the files and flipped it over.

At the bottom, stamped in red:

DESTINATION: Juarez, MX.

The silence that followed was electric.

Barry straightened. "We're not just dealing with a trafficking ring. We're standing in the middle of their old logistics hub."

Claire's voice dropped. "And Chloe nearly vanished trying to prove it."

Eric nodded grimly. "Not anymore. Now it's our turn."

Claire paused. "Did you hear that?"

Eric stilled beside her. "What?"

A muffled thump. Faint. Almost imagined.

Barry raised his hand, motioning for silence.

There it was again. A scuffling sound, this time from the back corner of the room—behind a toppled cabinet and a tarp-draped stack of boxes.

Claire moved before anyone could stop her, flashlight beam jittering as she hurried toward the sound. Barry and Eric flanked her as she knelt and yanked at the edge of the tarp.

Something moved underneath.

Then a desperate kick.

"Oh no!" Claire breathed. She dropped to her knees and pulled the tarp away.

There, bound and gagged, eyes wide and pleading, was Chloe.

She was pale, wrists raw from struggling, her mouth covered in duct tape. She thrashed as soon as she saw Claire, a muffled scream breaking through her lips.

"Chloe!" Claire's voice cracked as she reached for the tape. "It's okay, it's okay, we've got you."

Eric crouched to help, gently cutting through the zip ties that bound her ankles and wrists with his pocketknife while Barry kept watch, eyes sharp for any sign of ambush.

As soon as the gag was off, Chloe gasped for air. "It's a trap. They're watching—"

Barry's head snapped toward the entrance. "Move. Now."

"No," Chloe grabbed Claire's wrist, her grip surprisingly strong. "Not just watching. Listening. They know I know. They'll come back."

Claire cradled her sister, brushing tangled hair from her face. "We're taking you home."

Barry grabbed the tarp and slung it over his shoulder. "And whatever they were willing to hurt her to hide."

Eric scanned the room one last time, then spotted something near where Chloe had been hidden, a canvas pouch, duct-taped shut, half-buried under a box.

He picked it up. "We take this, too."

Barry opened it quickly. Inside were papers—wire transfers, names, birth certificates, addresses.

Claire's eyes flicked over the contents. "Some of these girls were from the shelter."

Barry's jaw tightened. "And some are from El Paso."

Chloe's voice, hoarse, whispered, "It's bigger than just the shelter. They're moving people. Like cargo."

Eric placed a hand on Claire's back. She didn't cry. She didn't speak. But her eyes locked on Chloe's, alive with fury and determination.

"We end this," Claire said.

Barry nodded. "We scan everything. Secure it. And then we go hunting."

Claire's hand slid into Eric's, grounding herself in the warmth of his grip. She stood, Chloe leaning against her, weak but safe.

Eric whispered, "We'll figure it out. Together."

Claire nodded, eyes locked on the exit.

"No," she said quietly. "We fight."

And they stepped into the night, carrying proof, purpose, and finally, each other.

* * *

By the time they returned to the penthouse, the sun disappeared behind the skyline. The air outside had cooled, but Eric felt heat building under his skin, the kind that came from knowing the next move mattered more than anything that came before.

He shut the front door behind them when Barry carried Chloe to one of the guest bedrooms. She refused to go to the hospital and get checked out, so Eric got the nurse for Beatrice to look her over. Chloe was fine but needed rest. The during the last check up, she was sleeping. It was too soon to let the rest of the family know she was here.

Claire moved like she was on autopilot, straight to the dining table, where they spread out Chloe's journals. She laid the bundle down beside them and began unpacking its contents carefully, as if afraid one wrong movement might erase Chloe's notes.

Barry followed behind, calm as ever, but Eric saw it, the way he rolled his shoulders once, the way his eyes scanned the corners of the room like someone still expecting danger. Something had shifted in Eric, too.

Eric peeled off his jacket and stepped into the kitchen, returning a moment later with a glass of water. Claire took it silently. Her hands were steady now, but her face was pale.

They spread everything out.

The list of names. And then the scraps: clipped screenshots, bits of conversation Chloe must've printed from a burner account. One page showed a series of transaction notes, coded, but familiar to Eric's trained eye. They weren't random.

They were payments.

Barry leaned over the table. "These transfers aren't small. Five-figure deposits. Offshore accounts.

Claire pointed to a date. "That's two days before she left Houston."

Claire looked up. "I don't see anything about the green truck. She mentioned it more than once in the journals."

Eric nodded slowly. "She was tracking someone connected to this."

Barry tapped the paper. "More than one someone. Look at all these names." he pointed to Chloe's scribbles.

Eric sat down beside her. "Chloe wasn't just running. She noticed people missing from the shelter and was trying to find them."

Barry nodded. "And drawing heat. Whoever she was watching, whoever they connected to, knew she was getting close, but they didn't kill her. Instead, they left her in that shed."

Claire stared at the list of names. "I recognize some from the shelter's check-in logs. She must have made a copy of every red flag."

Eric picked up the bundle, stared at the duct-tape residue like it might reveal more. "This file is through. She built it on her own. Pretty good work."

Claire looked up at him then, and the weight in her eyes hit him square in the chest. "She was always great at managing data."

A silence settled over the table, thick and full of questions.

Barry gathered half the documents and disappeared into the hallway towards his suite on the other side of the penthouse, already dialing. "I'm going to study this stuff closely in my suite. Y'all stay here and rest up. Tomorrow promises to be as crazy as today."

Eric stayed in the living room with Claire, easing into the silence of the room.

Claire sat still, "I thought she left because of something she did," she said quietly. "But it wasn't that. It was something she uncovered."

Eric didn't answer right away. He reached over retaking Claire's hand.

"I think Chloe is braver than any of us realized."

Claire smiled faintly, but her eyes shimmered. "She always was."

He hesitated, then reached up and tucked a loose curl of hair behind her ear. Her breath caught. She didn't move.

"I meant what I said earlier," he murmured. "This isn't just your fight anymore."

Her voice was soft. "It feels like ours."

He nodded once, eyes never leaving hers.

"You're not alone in this, Claire."

And for once, she didn't argue.

She simply leaned in, rested her head against his shoulder, and whispered, "Then let's not waste time."

Eric looked down at their hands as they embraced.

"Tomorrow," he said. "Chloe can tell us what she was chasing."

Claire didn't answer.

But the way she gripped his hand told him everything.

* * *

The penthouse was finally quiet.

Not the awkward silence of strangers cohabiting. Not the tense hush of unspoken truths. But something heavier. More intimate.

Earned.

Eric stood at the window, nursing a glass of whiskey, the city's lights flickering like Morse code across the skyline. Behind him, Claire disappeared into the guest room after they spent hours talking about random stuff. He felt her presence even from across the apartment, like gravity.

He hadn't said it aloud, but he knew now.

Eric's motive wasn't about helping Chloe anymore.

It was about holding on to Claire.

The sound of soft footsteps padded across the hardwood. He didn't turn. He didn't need to.

"You always drink alone?" Claire's voice was low, softer than usual.

"Only when it's quiet enough to think," Eric replied. "Which doesn't happen often these days."

She stepped beside him, wrapped in one of his hoodies, her hair damp from a shower. She smelled like his soap and her coffee. A combination that was already starting to wreck him.

"I couldn't sleep," she said.

"Neither could I."

Claire looked out over the city. Her smile was small but real. "My family thinks I am the boring sister."

"You're not," Eric said, voice lower now. "You're the one who holds everything together. You're the one people trust. That's not boring, it's terrifying.

Claire's eyes lifted to his.

"You sound like you're speaking from experience."

"I've been around a lot of people who pretend to be strong," Eric said. "But you? You don't pretend."

She held his gaze. "And you? Do you pretend?"

He stepped closer. "I used to. Until you."

The space between them narrowed. His hand brushed her wrist, and when she didn't pull away, he slipped his fingers into hers. Her pulse leapt under his touch.

"I don't know what we are," she whispered, "but I keep thinking about that kiss."

Eric took another step. Her breath hitched.

"I keep thinking about you," he said.

Her eyes flicked to his lips.

"I haven't wanted anyone in a long time," she said. "Not really. Not like this."

He didn't answer with words.

Instead, he leaned in, slowly, deliberately, giving her every chance to move. She didn't.

Their lips met, tentative at first, but then deeper. Hungrier. Her hand slid to his chest, and his fingers curled around her waist, pulling her against him.

It wasn't gentle anymore. It was need, pent-up, electric, and overwhelming.

She broke the kiss just long enough to whisper, "This is crazy."

"Yeah," he murmured, brushing his mouth against her neck, "but it's the only part that feels true right now."

Claire's fingers tugged at the hem of his shirt. His hands found her hips. They backed toward the sofa, tangled in each other, mouths meeting again with more urgency.

She gasped softly as he kissed her jaw, her pulse thundering beneath his lips.

"I don't want this to be a mistake," she said, her voice low and breathless.

"It's not," Eric replied. "Tell me to stop, and I will."

But she didn't say stop.

Instead, she kissed him again, deeper this time, hands curling into his shirt like she needed something to hold onto.

They reached the edge of the sofa. Claire sank back, pulling him with her. Eric slid between her legs. It was happening.

And just as he slid his hand under the hem of her hoodie,

BANG.

The front door burst open.

"CLAIRE!" Camila's voice rang out like a fire alarm.

Claire shoved Eric off her and bolted upright, breathless, hair askew. Eric landed halfway between her and the coffee table, groaning.

Camila stood in the entryway, arms crossed, a bag of flaming hot cheese puffs in one hand and a tablet in the other.

"Have you been ignoring your texts?!"

Claire blinked. "Camila. It's midnight."

"I texted you that Olivia put a Pop-Tart in the DVD player and now Netflix is broken!"

Eric rubbed his face. "There are so many things wrong with that sentence."

Camila ignored him and marched in like she owned the place. "Also, someone locked the wine drawer downstairs. Rude."

Claire stood, pulling the hoodie tighter around herself and trying to reclaim oxygen. "Camila, unless someone is bleeding or on fire, you can handle it."

"I am handling it," Camila sniffed. "Just wanted to let you know I'm suffering."

Claire turned to Eric with a strangled look.

He gave her a wry smile and leaned back against the sofa, voice dry. "Remind me to change the code for the door."

Camila flounced out with a toss of her hair and a loud crunch of cheese puffs.

The door clicked shut behind her.

Silence.

Claire looked down at Eric.

He was still sprawled on the rug, one hand on his chest like he was catching his breath. "Well. That was a moment."

Claire groaned and dropped onto the sofa beside him. "We were this close."

He smirked. "I remember."

She leaned back, breath finally settling. "If she ruins one more thing, I'm legally disowning her."

Eric nudged her thigh with his. "Next time, we find a private room and lock the door."

Claire gave him a side glance, her smile returning, lazy, wicked, promising. "Next time?"

He brushed her hair back from her cheek. "Definitely next time."

Chapter 15

Chloe

The scent of coffee was the first thing Chloe noticed when she stirred awake overhearing the quiet hum of an air conditioner. For a moment, she didn't know where she was. Then the events from the day before filtered in: the warehouse, the rescue, the overwhelming warmth of her sister's arms around her.

She sat up slowly, the guest room dimly lit with morning light sneaking in through the drawn curtains. Every muscle in her body ached like she'd gone ten rounds with a truck, and the truck won. Her wrists were sore, her shoulders stiff, her ribs tender from being curled up in a space not meant for anyone, let alone a human being. But she was alive. And safe. For now.

The sheets were too soft, the mattress too plush, nothing like the borrowed mattress pad she'd been crashing on at the shelter. Everything around her felt too still, too quiet, like a luxury hotel in a dream she hadn't paid for.

She slid out of bed and padded over to the window. The curtains were heavy, textured linen, a muted gray that barely moved in the air-conditioned breeze. With a slight tug, she peeled them open.

The breath caught in her throat.

This place wasn't just a high-rise. It was a *fortress*. A sleek, impenetrable tower that had wrapped Chloe in quiet and pulled her out of the dark.

"Hell," she whispered to no one. "Someone traded up."

And for the first time in weeks, something inside her, tight and wound and ready to snap, loosened just a bit.

Barefoot, Chloe padded out of the room, the plush carpet sinking softly beneath her toes. She paused at the door, glancing down at herself. She didn't remember changing out of her clothes. Didn't remember much after the adrenaline crash, but here she was, wrapped in a pair of borrowed pajamas: pale gray with tiny, embroidered stars at the cuffs, soft enough to feel like clouds. They looked like something her older sister, Claire, would pick, comfort disguised as elegance.

The fabric smelled faintly of lavender detergent and something familiar. Homey, in a way that twisted a lump into her throat.

The penthouse was silent in that expensive way, thick walls and too much space, where even her breathing felt like an intrusion. There were no creaky floorboards here, no TV murmuring in another room, no heavy footsteps stomping from one end of a cluttered hallway to the next. Just the faint clink of dishes, the low rumble of voices, and the distant, perfect hum of an HVAC system worth more than her last car.

She followed the sound like a thread, the warmth of it pulling her toward something she hadn't felt in a long time, comfort. Maybe even belonging.

The hallway opened into the living room and then the kitchen, a sun-drenched expanse of marble and chrome that looked lifted from a magazine. The scent of coffee hit Chloe first, rich and sharp, laced with something sweet and spiced.

Claire stood near the marble island; one hand wrapped around a tall iced brown sugar oat milk espresso with salted caramel foam. The cup, filled to the brim with amber swirls and cold foam clouds, handcrafted by a barista who moonlighted as a magician.

Of course.

Claire always had a fancy order: complicated, precise, and impossible to replicate without a paragraph of instructions. It suited her, Chloe thought. Claire always found comfort in control, in small luxuries that made life just a little more bearable.

The guy she saw with Claire at the coffee shop, didn't she call him Eric? Why did he look so familiar? He was perched on a barstool nearby, one bare foot tucked under the opposite knee, a soft charcoal hoodie slouched over his frame like it had been lived in for years.

The sweatpants he wore, designer probably, made him look even more relaxed, though his posture gave him away. One hand rested on his thigh, fingers tapping out a slow, thoughtful rhythm. His hair, slightly mussed, like he'd run his hand through it a dozen times already that morning. He looked normal. Maybe even tired. A little guarded. But present. Did he own this place, or was it his strong friend?

The other man leaned against the counter across from them, arms folded over his chest. His stance was casual but unmistakably alert, like a panther resting in the sun, but ready to pounce at the slightest noise. His sharp eyes flicked to Chloe the moment she entered, tracking her, taking in every movement. Not in a threatening way. Protective. Professional. But there was something softer in his gaze too: relief, maybe, or understanding. Chloe couldn't tell.

The whole scene struck her as surreal. Perhaps she'd stepped into a different life, a safer one. A cleaner one with no scars under the sleeves of borrowed pajamas, no constant weight pressing down on her chest.

And for a moment, she didn't know if she wanted to cry or ask someone to pour her a cup of coffee and pretend none of it ever happened.

The moment she entered, three pairs of eyes turned to her.

"Well," Chloe said, her voice rough, dry from disuse. "Good morning to me."

Claire moved first, rushing over and wrapping her in a tight hug. "You slept through breakfast with the kids. We didn't want to wake you."

"No problem. I'm not ready to see them yet," Chloe mumbled into her sister's hair.

Claire let go, brushing a stray curl behind her ear. "Come on. Sit. You hungry?"

"More like caffeinated curious," Chloe said, stepping past her and heading for the espresso machine like it was an old friend she hadn't seen in a while.

Claire's cup was already on the counter, tall and glistening. Chloe picked it up, sniffed it cautiously, then made a face. "Still into dessert for breakfast, I see."

"I like what I like," Claire replied, no shame at all.

Chloe shook her head and started building her preferred drink—just milk, coffee, and a touch of sugar. A plain latte. Simple. Steady. Something she could control when nothing else made sense.

As the machine hissed and steamed behind her, she became aware of two sets of eyes still watching.

Claire noticed. "Right—Chloe, I don't think you've formally met our very unexpected housemates."

Chloe turned, latte in hand, and Claire gestured between the two men.

"This is Eric Whiff," she said, voice gentling just slightly. "And… he's something special to me."

Eric moved then, almost instinctively, stepping in beside Claire like her words drew him there. He didn't touch her, but the air between them seemed to change—less space, more gravity.

Chloe tilted her head, clocking the shift instantly. "Huh. The tech guy? Billionaire with a tragic dating history and an absurdly good PR team?"

Eric lifted his cup in a half-salute. "Guilty. Though I like to think I'm slightly more complex than my ChatGPT results."

Chloe smirked. "We'll see."

Claire tried not to smile too much but failed.

She turned to the man still leaning against the counter. "And this is Barry Poet. He's Eric's head of security and the reason we found you when we did."

Chloe gave Barry a long look. "Poet? That's a real name?"

Barry's lips twitched. "Unfortunately for me, yes."

"He's also the one who got us into that shed," Claire added. "He jimmied the lock like it was nothing."

Chloe's eyes widened slightly. "Nice. Always wanted to be rescued by a guy with a noir detective name and a B&E skillset."

Barry gave a slow, respectful nod. "Some doors don't need kicking, just persuasion."

With introductions complete, Chloe slid onto one of the kitchen stools and took her first long sip of the latte. Warm. Grounding. Her fingers wrapped tightly around the mug as if it anchored her.

She looked between the three of them, a hint of suspicion still in her voice. "So, I guess someone better catch me up."

They waited just long enough for her to exhale before they started to talk.

Barry began. "We tracked you from the shelter when we found the first journal you left. When your name popped on an encrypted message thread, we realized the threat wasn't theoretical anymore."

Eric jumped in, not even trying to mask the worry in his voice. "When Claire told me what was going on, we worked with Barry's team to trace you. We followed the breadcrumbs you left. The journal, the camera footage, the cash trail. We almost missed the storage shed."

"I'm glad you didn't." Chloe swallowed hard. "It wasn't just about me. I was scared they'd go after Claire. Or Camila. Or Mom."

"You did the right thing, Chloe," Barry said firmly. "Now we can protect you."

She glanced around the penthouse, noting the piles of suitcases, kids' toys, and an empty cat carrier someone had shoved in the corner. "Seems like you're protecting all of us."

Eric shrugged. "Your family moved in and took over. I've resigned myself to being the reluctant host of a very chaotic sleepover."

Chloe grinned. "You don't seem the sleepover type."

He smiled faintly. "I wasn't."

Claire leaned against the counter beside Barry. "We've got a lot to figure out. But we're not doing it alone anymore."

Chloe took another sip of her latte. The warmth seeped through her fingers, down to the bone.

"I should've told you sooner," she said softly.

Claire reached across the island and grabbed her hand. "You can tell us now. That's what matters."

* * *

They sat in the sun-drenched kitchen, the silence wrapping around them like a weighted blanket.

Chloe stared into the depths of her latte, her fingers tight around the cup. The warmth had faded, but she wasn't ready to let go of it. Claire sat across from her, eyes soft and steady. Eric leaned against the counter again, silent but attentive. Barry sat at the end of the island, arms loose now, but his focus hadn't wavered since she started talking.

She took a breath.

"It started right after I left the recovery center. I was clean for six months. Tired. Broke. But I didn't want to come crawling home, not like that. I wanted, I don't know, something that felt like redemption."

Claire nodded, her hands folded on the counter, as if holding herself together.

"I found work at a shelter downtown," Chloe continued. "They didn't pay, but they gave me a bed. All I had to do was handle intake records, names, ID checks, simple stuff. At first, it was fine. Hard. Messy. But real. Most people just needed a place to breathe."

Her gaze drifted toward the window, where the city skyline shimmered in the late morning light.

"But then I started noticing things. People who usually stayed for weeks were suddenly gone after a night. No word, no follow-up. I asked questions, got shrugs. I was brushed off."

She looked back at them, eyes sharper now.

"There was a mom and her little boy. I'd been trying to help them get stable housing. She was sober. Trying. But one morning, they were gone. No warning. When I pulled her file, it was updated to say she relapsed. That she left on her own. But I *know* she didn't."

"What happened next?" Barry asked, voice calm, measured.

Chloe's throat tightened. "I brought it up to Delia. That's the woman who ran the shelter. I told her something didn't feel right. She smiled like I'd complimented her shoes. Then she leaned in and told me I should be careful. That 'people like me' don't usually survive the weight of their past coming back around."

Claire inhaled sharply.

"I thought she was bluffing," Chloe said. "Until I started seeing this green truck outside. Parked across the street. Always running. Always waiting. Then one night, I saw Delia walk a young woman, barely older than a teenager, out of the shelter and toward it. She looked terrified."

Eric frowned. "You followed them?"

"I tried. I slipped into Delia's office and found these addresses all over Texas. The Google Maps images were blurry and old, so I went myself when I had time off. I borrowed cars from people I knew, or I caught a bus. I kept noting the green truck when I saw it. The windows were tinted so that I couldn't see in, and no one ever came out. I didn't know what I was doing, but I couldn't let it go."

She paused, staring down at the counter.

"Then it got worse. Delia cornered me after a shift. She said she knew everything. My history. My sisters' names. Where my mother lived, she threatened that if I didn't stop asking questions, my family would start disappearing too."

Claire's lips parted, her hands curling into fists. Eric took a step closer to her.

"That's when I left. I grabbed what I could, vanished. But I kept watching for the truck. I knew something was happening. I just couldn't prove it."

Barry's voice was low, but steady. "And they found you."

Chloe nodded. "Yeah. I was staying in a cheap motel out by the loop, watching a warehouse where the truck kept showing up. I must've gotten too close. Someone grabbed me when I stepped out to get food. Next thing I knew, I was in that storage shed. No idea where I was. I didn't even know if anyone was coming."

She exhaled, shaky and slow. "They didn't ask questions. They didn't demand anything. They just left me there. Like I wasn't worth the trouble. I think they were going to come back and finish it."

Barry's jaw flexed. Claire looked like she wanted to cry and scream at the same time.

Chloe looked at each of them in turn. "If you hadn't shown up when you did—if you were even an hour later…"

She didn't finish the sentence. She didn't need to.

Claire stood and moved around the island, pulling Chloe into a hug. Not tentative. Not careful. Fierce.

"You're safe now," Claire whispered into her hair. "We've got you."

For a moment, Chloe let herself believe it.

* * *

The kids were the first to spot her.

Nathan gasped from the hallway and vanished, calling out like it was Christmas morning. A stampede of feet followed, and within seconds, the living room erupted with squeals.

"Aunt Chloe!"

"Are you okay?"

"You look different!"

Olivia launched herself into Chloe's arms, nearly knocking her off balance. Henry barreled in next, followed by Nathan, who hung back just a moment before joining the group hug. Chloe laughed, a sound that cracked mid-chest, as she held them all close.

"I missed you, little monsters."

"You're *so* skinny," Olivia said, studying her like she was a stranger and a celebrity all at once.

"You smell like coffee," Henry added.

Nathan tilted his head. "Where did you go?"

Before she could answer, the elevator chimed and the doors slid open.

Camila's voice rang out before she even stepped into the penthouse. "Chloe Eidean, *what in the hell—*"

She charged forward, dramatic as ever, her robe barely tied and one slipper half off. Her eyes swept over Chloe, and her mouth fell open mid-sentence.

"You're... *alive?*"

Chloe straightened. "Hi."

Camila stopped a few feet away. Her face twisted through several stages—shock, fury, relief—before settling on a scowl.

"You let us think you were dead! You didn't call. You didn't send a *text*. You let me explain to the kids that their aunt might have overdosed again!"

"I had to," Chloe said quietly.

Claire stepped in, her voice gentle but firm. "Camila—"

"No. She doesn't get to show up in your borrowed pajamas, wrapped in mystery, acting like this is normal."

"I was trying to protect you," Chloe said, her voice steady.

"By *disappearing?*"

Chloe met her eyes. "By not getting you killed."

That landed. Camila's expression flickered, something behind her bravado cracking open.

"I know I hurt you," Chloe added. "And I'm sorry. Truly. But this time, I wasn't running from myself—I was running toward something dangerous so it wouldn't touch you."

Camila blinked. Her jaw clenched. And then, in true Camila fashion, she threw her arms around Chloe and squeezed so tight it nearly knocked the breath from her lungs.

"If you ever do that again," she muttered into Chloe's shoulder, "I will *actually* murder you."

Chloe smiled through the burn in her eyes. "Noted."

Claire stepped up and wrapped her arms around both of them, and soon the kids pressed in, forming a knot of family that was messy, loud, and real. From the side of her eye, Chloe caught Claire's hand reach out of the pile of people towards Eric, who hesitated at first, but then grabbed her hand and was pulled in. Did Chloe also see a smile cross Barry's face?

After a moment, Claire pulled back and said softly, "Come on. There's someone else who needs to see you."

Chloe followed her to the private elevator, riding in silence as her nerves twisted. When they stepped out onto the lower level, the air felt warmer, more lived-in. Toys were strewn in a corner. A cat bed was perched beneath a sunny window. It smelled like ginger tea and family.

Claire led her into the back room where Beatrice sat in her chair near the window, a crocheted shawl draped over her shoulders, her locket in hand. The light caught the edges of her silver hair.

She looked up slowly—and saw her.

Chloe stopped in the doorway, frozen.

"Hi, Mama," she whispered.

Beatrice's face softened. Her eyes welled. Her lips trembled, but she didn't speak. Her hand lifted in a slow, deliberate gesture—beckoning.

Chloe moved forward, knees buckling as she dropped beside her. She laid her head gently in her mother's lap, careful not to jostle her, and let herself be held.

Beatrice's hand trembled as it found Chloe's curls, brushing through them like she used to when they were girls and someone had a nightmare.

"I told you," Chloe whispered. "That night… I told you everything through the window. I didn't know if you could hear me."

Beatrice tapped the locket once, then pressed it to her chest.

She had heard. Every word.

And for the first time in months, Chloe felt anchored.

* * *

Back upstairs, the tone had shifted. Claire sat on the couch; Oliver curled into her side. Henry was explaining something to Nathan that required dramatic hand gestures and at least three unnecessary facts.

And in the middle of it all was Eric.

He wasn't loud. He didn't demand space. But Chloe noticed how he handed Camila a fresh towel without being asked; how he refilled Claire's drink and took her empty glass, how he replaced a bulb that had been flickering over the kitchen island. He moved like someone used to making space for others, someone who didn't mind stepping aside if it meant someone else could breathe.

Not flashy. Not performative. Just there.

And more than that, *present*.

Chloe watched him for a long moment and then looked at Claire, who didn't say anything, just smiled softly when their eyes met.

But then Chloe's gaze shifted—toward the far end of the room.

Barry was standing near the window, phone in hand, speaking in low tones. His shoulders were tense, but there was something calm in the way he moved. Protective. Grounded. Sharp.

She hadn't looked at him before. Not properly.

But now, in the comfort of sunlight and safety, she did.

And something in her stirred.

It wasn't just gratitude.

It was interest.

And it surprised her.

Chapter 16

Claire

The penthouse had finally gone still. No laughter, no arguing, no cartoons echoing from the living room. Just the hum of distant city lights and the soft shuffle of fabric as Claire stood at the edge of the bed, wearing one of Eric's T-shirts. It fell mid-thigh, worn and soft, with the faintest scent of his cologne clinging to the collar. When she did her laundry, his tees kept getting mixed up with her clothes. They were the perfect sleep shirt.

Behind her, the bedroom door clicked shut. Then the lock turned.

She glanced over her shoulder.

Eric stood by the door, shirtless, sweatpants slung low on his hips, his expression dark and unreadable.

"I locked it this time," he said, voice low and taut.

Claire lifted a brow. "Expecting company?"

"Expecting Camila to burst in asking if we've seen her charger again," he said, walking toward her slowly. "And hoping you'd let me stay. Here. With you."

That last sentence stopped her.

She turned, heart stammering a little. "Stay tonight?"

He shook his head. "Stay. Period. Through all of it. I know I messed up the first version of us—online or otherwise—but this—" he closed the space between them and gently touched the hem of her shirt, "—this feels like the only real thing I've had in a long time."

Claire swallowed hard, her throat thick with emotion. "You're asking permission?"

"I want to be in this with you. But only if you want it too."

She didn't speak right away. Instead, she reached up, curling her hand behind his neck, drawing his forehead down to rest against hers. "Then what are you waiting for?"

That was all he needed.

The kiss came fast—hungry, unspoken tension finally breaking loose. His hands gripped her waist, thumbs sliding under the hem of her shirt as she rose on her toes to meet him. Her fingers tangled in his hair, pulling him deeper, anchoring him as her body lit with heat.

Eric guided her back, her legs brushing the bed. His mouth never left hers as she fell into the sheets, pulling him with her. The weight of him, the scent of him, everything—*finally*—was hers to feel.

His lips moved along her jaw, down her throat. She arched into him, breath ragged, wanting more. Needing more.

"I haven't stopped thinking about you since that first message," he whispered into her skin. "And every second since."

Claire opened her mouth to respond—then—

Knock.

Sharp. Intentional.

They both froze.

Eric groaned into her neck. "You've got to be kidding me."

Another knock. Louder.

Barry's voice, clear through the door. "Apologies. But it's urgent."

Claire fell back against the pillow, breathless and swearing under it. "He's going to be single-handedly responsible for my celibacy. That is it. I think I love you, but the universe has spoken. Put a ring on it."

Eric sat up, dragging a hand through his hair. "Got it. And I *locked* the damn door."

Claire grabbed the sheet, wrapping it around herself. "Go. Before he breaks in."

Eric stood, half-dressed, frustration simmering in every muscle as he opened the door.

Barry stood there, unfazed by Eric's appearance. "Green truck. Circling three blocks out. They've been stationary for twenty minutes. We think they're watching. Possibly waiting."

Claire sat up straighter, instincts already firing.

Barry's gaze flicked from Eric to her. "It's starting again. And we don't have the luxury of pretending otherwise."

Eric looked back at Claire, tension still in his frame—but his expression had changed. Focused now. Protective.

She gave a tight nod.

Game on.

∗ ∗ ∗

The lock had barely clicked shut when Barry turned and started down the hall, already ten steps ahead. Claire stood for a moment, pulse still pounding from the way Eric's mouth had just been on her skin—now replaced by the unmistakable weight of reality setting back in.

Eric ran a hand through his hair, the last flickers of warmth draining from his expression. "I'll get dressed."

"Me too," she said, already crossing to the closet in the guest suite.

She changed quickly into black leggings, her most neutral hoodie, and a pair of boots that somehow managed to make it into her suitcase when she packed. She tied her hair into a quick ponytail, grabbed her phone and met Eric outside the suite as he emerged in dark jeans, a navy thermal shirt, and the look of a man preparing for battle.

No more intimacy. No more quiet.

Only motion.

Barry hadn't said *where* to meet him, but Claire already knew. There was only one space in the penthouse Barry consistently kept off-limits—the suite that had once belonged to one of Eric's top advisors, then later converted for Barry when he took over security detail full-time.

They followed the hallway past the library, through the study, and down a narrow corridor that ended at an unmarked door.

Eric knocked once. The door clicked open.

Barry stood inside, already geared up, black jacket half-zipped and an earpiece clipped in. But what caught Claire off guard wasn't him, it was the room itself.

The suite was transformed.

It looked like a private command post filled with a sleek U-shaped desk setup surrounded by monitors. A wall-mounted screen showed live exterior feeds—sidewalks, garages, traffic intersections. A whiteboard hung with names and strings of hand-sketched maps. In one corner, a cot was folded against the wall. In another, a stack of duffel bags sat zipped and ready. One monitor blinked with GPS routes, another split between infrared building scans and a list of encrypted messages.

Claire blinked. "Fancy."

Barry glanced at her. "I upgraded a bit when I realized everyone was included in the cross-hairs."

Eric moved to the desk and leaned in. "How long have you been running this?

Barry didn't answer immediately. Instead, he pulled up the latest footage on the main screen. The green truck, low-res and washed in shadows, circled the building once—twice—then disappeared off the feed.

Barry tapped the screen again, then leaned in, frowning.

"They're adapting," he said. "Second pass through the building was tighter. Not external recon, interior mapping. Someone's already breached protocol."

Claire moved beside him, arms folding tightly. "Anything about the names from the journals? What about Delia?"

Barry's jaw tensed. "Intercepted traffic names her. 'Clean removal.' It wasn't about catching Chloe—it was a trigger. If they failed, they escalate from surveillance to action."

Eric stepped in, eyes sharp. "So what's the plan? We evacuate?"

Barry shook his head. "No. This place is secure—more secure than anywhere else in Houston. But it only works if we know who's inside."

He tapped a few more keys. The screen switched to a paused camera feed: a woman in a city maintenance uniform, pushing a utility cart down a side hallway.

Claire stepped closer, blinking. "Wait. Who is that? She doesn't look like the others I have seen since I have been here."

"Delia Hart," Chloe said grimly from the doorway. She was already dressed, hair pulled back. "She was working intake at the shelter. I'd recognize that walk anywhere."

"She got in six hours ago," Barry muttered. "Falsified contractor credentials. Our lockdown system's solid, but she used a legacy backdoor—one of the old override codes we never replaced on the first floor."

Eric cursed under his breath. "Then she's already here."

Barry looked up. "Which means we don't leave. We lock it down. Now."

Claire and Chloe tried to text and call Camila to no avail. They sprinted down the stairwell to the apartment below, using Eric's code to get in. After banging on Camilia's door for what felt like hours, she opened her door in a silk robe, half asleep.

"What is happening?" she demanded.

"No time," Claire said, brushing past. "Wake the kids. Everyone stays in this room. Don't open the door for anyone besides one of us, no matter what you hear. Understand?"

Camila scoffed. "Excuse me—"

Chloe turned, eyes blazing. "There is a woman in this building who tried to have me killed. Do you want your kids to be next?"

That shut her up.

* * *

The air in Camilia's apartment felt thinner than it should have—like pressure was building from the inside. Morning light filtered in through the floor-to-ceiling windows, but the city below was just a hazy blur of motionless traffic and indistinct shapes. From this high up, there were no useful details—only distance.

Claire stood near the door, boots planted, hoodie zipped to her chin. Barry was already inside, his gear bag slung open across Camila's marble kitchen island, tablet propped against a cereal box left from last night.

"She's in the building," Barry said, tapping the screen. "Maybe the third floor, northeast quadrant. That section's under light renovation—perfect spot to stage and observe."

The apartment was an explosion of morning clutter—plastic bowls half-filled with cereal, juice boxes wedged between throw pillows, and a tiny Spock doll sitting on top of a makeshift couch fort. A poster of the USS Enterprise half rolled into a tube near the media cabinet, and a Starfleet insignia nightlight blinked blue and gold from a hallway plug.

Beatrice sat in a recliner in the living room, bundled in a thick knit blanket, a mug of now-cold chamomile tea resting on a tray beside her. Her gaze drifted around the room, trying to follow the motion of her daughters without speaking.

Chloe hovered protectively nearby. "We need to assume Delia's watching."

Eric stood at the window, arms folded. "We're too high up. If she's tracking us, it's through building systems, not line-of-sight."

Just then, Camila burst in from the hallway, hair frizzed, bathrobe half open over sweatpants printed with little red comets. Her youngest son was holding her hand, and her daughter trailed behind in a Starfleet uniform pajama set, clutching a Tribble plush.

"Can someone explain what the hell is going on?" Camila demanded. "You're all whispering like it's the end of the world, and I haven't even had coffee!"

Claire moved away from the window. "We've confirmed Delia Hart is in the building. Third floor. She got in hours ago. You really need to get everyone in one room or location. I don't care where."

Camila blinked. "She's here? In *this* building?"

"She hasn't reached this apartment," Barry said, sharp and steady. "But she's on the move. This space has one entry, one rear utility stairwell, and a dozen blind spots. She's likely heading up at some point."

Camila paled and directed her children to her room. "And where is the nurse? Beatrice was supposed to have her meds by now."

"Probably stalled. Or worse," Chloe muttered.

Barry pulled up the paused footage again—a woman in a nondescript cap and a contractor's vest stepping off the freight elevator. "That's her."

Claire exhaled hard. "So what's our next move?"

"We trap her," Barry said. "Eric, go back upstairs—run full building surveillance. Chloe, lock this unit down tight. Claire, you're with me. We'll hit the service corridor near the freight access and wait."

Camila stared, still trying to take it in. "And what am I supposed to do while you're off on a space-marine mission?"

"Keep the kids quiet. Stay with Beatrice. Don't open the door unless it's one of us." Barry said.

"And if she gets in here?" Camila asked, voice cracking.

Claire looked at her sister and softened just a little. "Then you do what you always do."

Camila lifted a brow. "What's that?"

"Improvise," Claire said. "And keep your crew alive."

Chloe walked past and locked the front door with a *click*. "Let's go."

Barry opened the hallway door. Claire gave Beatrice one last glance before following. Her mother blinked once, then slowly nodded—like she understood far more than she could say.

* * *

The plan had just begun to fall into motion—Barry tightening the strap on his pack, Eric heading toward the door, Chloe double-checking the lock—when the soft *ding* of the elevator reached Claire's ears.

Everyone froze.

A beat of silence.

Then—*a knock.*

Three sharp taps.

Barry turned to the wall panel and hit the intercom.

"Who is it?"

A garbled male voice came through. "Delivery for Eric Whiff. Supermart order—six bags."

Claire's brow furrowed. "What the hell? Camila, seriously? You ordered groceries with Eric's account again?"

"I didn't!" Camila shouted from the hallway.

"She did," Claire snapped. "This is exactly—"

"I didn't!" Camila yelled again, louder. "I swear on my Tribble collection, I didn't order anything!"

Eric's expression hardened. "My account's frozen. Has been for two days."

Barry's eyes flicked to the monitor. "Back away from the door. *Now.*"

"What?" Claire asked.

"*DUCK!*" Barry shouted.

The explosion hit an instant later.

A thunderous *pop*—small but sharp—blew the front lock apart. The door flew inward as three figures in black tactical gear burst through, weapons drawn, faces masked.

Camila screamed and ran for the hallway where her kids were hidden. Claire lunged instinctively toward her mother and sister, shouting, "Get down!"

Eric intercepted the first intruder, tackling him into the wall with a crack of drywall. The second rushed toward Barry, swinging a baton—Barry ducked the strike and slammed his shoulder into the man's gut, knocking him back.

Chloe grabbed a decorative lamp from the side table and hurled it, shattering it against one attacker's helmet. "Get the hell out of our house!"

Claire hit the floor, rolled toward Beatrice, and grabbed the armrest of her mother's chair to pull her back. "We have to move—now!"

Beatrice's eyes were wide, wild—but focused.

"Stay with me, Mama," Claire whispered.

Across the room, Barry pulled a taser from his belt, aimed, and fired. The crackling pulse lit up the attacker's chest, sending him convulsing to the floor.

"Claire, now!" Barry barked.

Claire pulled Beatrice behind the overturned coffee table. She saw Eric punch another man so hard he went reeling into the TV stand, taking out a stack of Star Trek DVDs on the way down.

But the third attacker—uninjured—sprinted toward the back of the apartment.

"The service elevator!" Barry shouted, already giving chase.

Claire turned to find Chloe—she was running toward the hallway, dodging a low kick, trying to block the escape route.

Then—

The glint of a gun.

Drawn by the fleeing man as he reached the service corridor.

Everything slowed.

Claire's voice caught in her throat. *"CHLOE!"*

The shot cracked through the room like thunder.

And Beatrice stood.

Not stumbled.

Not fell.

Stood.

She rose from her wheelchair like gravity no longer applied and stepped into the line of fire—arms open, eyes calm.

The bullet hit her in the chest.

Claire screamed.

Time snapped forward. Barry tackled the shooter from behind, slamming him face-first into the door frame. The man dropped the gun and bolted down the corridor, disappearing into the elevator shaft. The others followed—running, injured, retreating.

Silence fell in the aftermath, broken only by Beatrice's soft gasp.

Claire crawled across the floor, blood roaring in her ears.

"Mama—Mama—no, no, no—"

Beatrice was still standing, somehow. Her knees gave just as Claire caught her. Together, they crumpled gently to the floor.

Chloe reached them next, her hands trembling.

Beatrice's lips moved. Claire leaned in.

"Protect her," she whispered. "Both of you."

Then her head tilted back, eyes fluttering closed, breath still.

Claire let out a raw, broken sound—not quite a cry, not quite a scream.

Eric dropped to his knees beside them.

Barry stood near the door, fists clenched, chest heaving.

The apartment was destroyed. Blood on the floor. The scent of gunpowder in the air. Shattered glass beneath their feet.

But the only thing Claire could see was her mother—still, strong, and now gone.

<h1 style="text-align:center">Chapter 17</h1>

Barry

The funeral was small.

Private.

Just family, a few friends, and a handful of people who knew Beatrice Eidean as more than a diagnosis. More than a burden or a chair or a whisper of the woman she used to be. Eric took care of everything, from cleaning up Camilia's apartment downstairs, to the funeral arrangements.

Barry stood at the back of the shaded garden, hands folded in front of him, sunglasses shielding his eyes from the late morning glare, and from the people who might notice him watching too closely. Eric stood beside Barry, letting everyone have their space to grieve and be available to help.

Barry hadn't expected the ache in his chest.

Beatrice had barely spoken, hadn't walked in years. But she had stood when it mattered. Stood when he hadn't. When he couldn't.

And now she was gone.

He shifted his weight slightly and glanced toward the front row.

Claire sat between Chloe and Camila; fingers laced tightly with her sisters.' Her face was calm, but Barry knew the tremble behind her stillness. He'd seen it the night before, when she sat on the floor beside her mother's empty chair long after the paramedics had come and gone. When she wouldn't let go of Chloe's hand even as she answered calls and signed papers and told the world she was fine.

But it was Chloe who caught Barry's attention now.

Not the same Chloe he'd guarded. Not the wild-eyed ghost who stumbled into the safehouse with a flash drive and a death wish. This Chloe sat tall. Her eyes dry. Her presence rooted.

Strong.

And it hit Barry harder than he expected. He wasn't looking at someone he needed to protect anymore

He was just looking at her.

Not as a threat, or an asset, or a variable to manage.

But as a woman who had survived something almost no one would ever understand. Who had risked her name and her life for strangers and still showed up for her family with blood on her sleeves and tears dried before they fell.

He should've noticed earlier. Maybe he had.

But when you're focused on shielding people, you don't always see them clearly.

Now he did.

A breeze moved through the trees, rustling the white ribbon tied to the back of Beatrice's empty chair. Claire's voice cracked as she read her mother's favorite poem, something about time folding inward and the weight of memory. Barry only caught pieces. He was too focused on the way Chloe's head dipped slightly when the last line hit:

"You were never gone, you were just holding the sky from behind."

The crowd began to rise.

Claire turned to walk toward the burial site with Camila at her side. Eric followed them closely.

Chloe stood last.

Barry stepped forward, just enough to meet her halfway.

"You okay?" he asked.

"No," she said. "But I will be."

Her voice was quiet, but clear. No tremble. No disguise.

Barry nodded. "You're not going back into hiding."

"No," Chloe said. "Not yet. I want to stay a little longer. Tie off the loose ends."

She met his eyes, and something flickered between them.

"Besides," she added, a faint smirk rising, "you're not that good at saying goodbye."

Barry chuckled softly. "No. I'm not."

They stood together for a moment as the mourners began to drift away.

And for once, Barry didn't feel like a bodyguard.

He felt like a man standing beside a woman who didn't need saving anymore.

And he wasn't entirely sure how to walk away from that.

* * *

The first sip hit like memory.

Sweet. Smooth. Salted caramel on the cold foam, brown sugar lingering in the oat milk. A drink Barry mocked, before Claire insisted, he try it "just once."

Now it was his usual.

Barry leaned back in the corner booth of Moody Grounds, letting the late afternoon hum of espresso machines and quiet conversation settle around him. His tablet rested on the table beside the coffee, unread. He wasn't here to work.

He was here because it was the first time in weeks, he'd been able to sit still.

No threats. No encrypted drives. No blood on his sleeves.

Just coffee.

He let his eyes wander around the café, polished wood tables, book-lined shelves, the same chipped ceramic sugar jar near the barista station. This place hadn't changed at all.

But everything else had.

He thought of Claire.

How the first time he saw her, she'd been standing at the counter, ordering this very drink, completely unaware that the man she was texting, Ethan Wells, was his boss.

She'd been sharp then. Guarded. Slightly annoyed by everything around her.

Now she was smiling more. Laughing with Eric in a way Barry hadn't seen anyone do since before the world learned his net worth.

They were dating now, openly, honestly, and without the screens between them. Barry had never seen either of them that happy. Not in the real way.

Not in the kind of way that quieted the rest of the world.

He took another sip and let the thought land:

Would I even recognize that feeling if it came my way?

He didn't date much. Didn't have time. Didn't want to risk getting attached to someone who couldn't handle the shadows that followed him. He originally planned to make his way back to Mobile and connect again with his team, but he could leave yet. Too many unresolved issues.

They were still tracking Crystal, but she disappeared from the grid. No sign anywhere and then there was the third gunman, the one who escaped the apartment. Barry had a personal score to settle with him.

But lately?

Lately, he wondered.

He stared into the swirl of foam at the top of his drink.

And then the bell above the front door chimed.

He didn't look up right away.

Not until the footsteps paused.

And then,

"Barry?"

He looked up.

And there she was.

Chloe.

No hoodie. No backpack. Just jeans and a soft olive-green shirt, hair pulled back, face clearer than he'd seen it in weeks.

They locked eyes.

For a second, neither moved.

Then, at the exact same time, they both smiled.

Not big. Not dramatic.

But real.

The kind that said I didn't expect this, but I'm glad it happened.

Barry stood, still holding his coffee. "Didn't think I'd see you again," he said, voice low.

Chloe stepped forward. "Me neither."

She glanced at his cup, then raised an eyebrow. "Let me guess, iced brown sugar oat milk with salted caramel cold foam?"

He grinned. "What can I say? You people have good taste."

She slid into the seat across from him, still smiling, "I am a Matcha with Mocha and Hazelnut kind of person, myself. It tastes like a milkshake."

No plans. No mission.

Just the sound of their drinks settling onto the table.

And the beginning of something neither of them had expected.

About the Author

Paula Lenor Webb is a writer, historian, and librarian whose work bridges fact and fiction with Southern charm and emotional depth. She is the author of both historical biographies and contemporary novels, including the *TruePair Series*. When she's not writing, Paula champions the arts and literacy through her work at the University of South Alabama and community initiatives like JAWSFest. *Not Another Swipe* is the first novel in her romantic suspense series exploring love, identity, and the power of unexpected connections.

Know anyone who can turn my book into a movie? I will pay you a finders fee!

Think about it and send me an email at plwebbie@gmail.com.

You can connect with me on:

🌐 https://plwebb.com

❑ https://www.facebook.com/plwebbie

Also by Paula Lenor Webb

Paula Webb's writing combines emotional depth, suspense, and rich character development. Her stories explore the complexities of relationships between family, lovers, and identity, set against both historical and contemporary backdrops. With a Southern voice and a librarian's precision, she crafts narratives that are as heart-pounding as they are heartfelt.

Vicksburg: Skirts to Swords Adventure
Vicksburg: A Skirts to Swords Adventure follows Rebecca Cashin, a daring young woman who disguises herself as a man to fight in the Civil War. As she navigates the dangers of espionage, battlefields, and forbidden love, Rebecca risks everything to protect freedom and her secret. A gripping tale of courage, identity, and sacrifice.

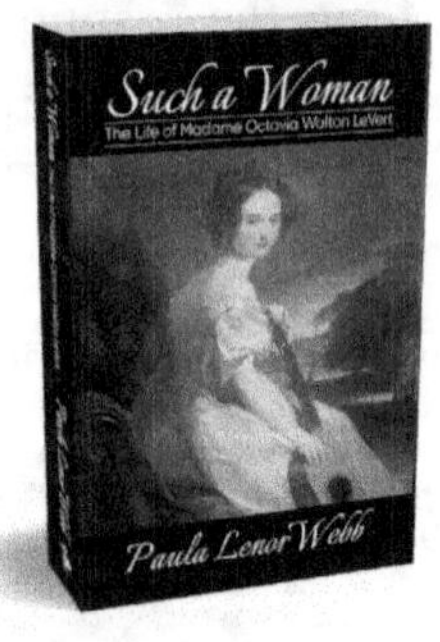

Such a Woman: The Life of Madame Octavia Walton LeVert
Such a Woman: The Life of Madame Octavia Walton LeVert tells the remarkable story of one of the South's most influential yet overlooked women. A celebrated author, socialite, and political hostess, Octavia Walton LeVert moved among presidents, poets, and foreign dignitaries—earning comparisons to Dolly Madison. Through meticulous research, Paula Webb brings to life this dynamic 19th-century figure who defied societal expectations and left a lasting cultural legacy in the American South.

Mr. Paris Makes a Mess: An Excelsior Band Murder Mystery

When the lifeless body of one of his former students tumbles out of a coffin in the middle of a funeral, Hashea Paris knows one thing for sure—something is terribly wrong. A jazz musician by trade and the charismatic leader of The Excelsior Band, Hashea has no business playing detective. And yet, with questions swirling and the whispers of murder in the air, he can't help but be drawn into the mystery.

Mississippi Mojo...And Murder: Tale of the Blues

A sixty-year-old cold case and a big city sheriff seeking redemption—it's time for the dead to rise. A thwarted youthful romance blends with the blues and Mama Cheche's mojo. Controversy ensues when a blues singer groom goes missing in Cleveland, Mississippi. All becomes a tangled web.

Devilry in the Delta: A Mississippi Mojo Thriller

Hunter Harley had a run of bad luck before he came to Cleveland, Mississippi as their new sheriff. Solving a sixty-year-old cold case murder had given him satisfaction and made his life better. Then, his nemesis, a serial killer also targeting Shannon Brown's two young children, stalks him. The hunter becomes the hunted. Could his new friends help him survive?

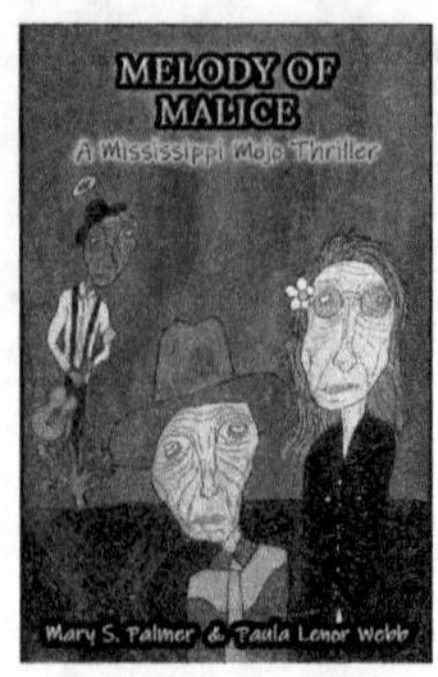

Melody of Malice: A Mississippi Mojo Thriller
When a narcissist, ruthless mother exploits her own children, Shannon, their half-sister, is hard-pressed to keep them safe from her wiles. Sheriff Hunter Harley comes to their aid but protecting them isn't an easy task.